DON'T CALL ME LOVE

Don't Call Me Love

Backyard Horse Tales #3

By

Jackie Anton

Illustrator

Sandy Shipley

COPYRIGHT INFO

Copyright © 2017 Jackie Anton

The moral rights of the author has ben asserted.

All rights reserved.

No part of this publication may be reproduced, stored in a retrieval system, or transmitted, in any form or by any means, without the written permission of the author/publisher, nor be otherwise circulated in any form of binding or cover other than that in which it is published and without a similar condition including this condition being imposed on the subsequent purchaser.

This book is a work of fiction . Places, events, and situations in this book are Purely fictional and any resemblance to persons, living or dead is coincidental.

Published by
Half Appy Press

ISBN: 978-0-9962645-7-0

Acknowledgments

Thank you to my daughter Pat for helping me shape up the first draft. The completion of this novel wouldn't have been possible without the support of my family and a wonderful friend, horsewoman, and super illustrator, Sandy Shipley.

A big hug is in order for my editor Adele Brinkley.

Table of Contents

Chapter	Page
1. Lazy Summer Days	1
2. New Herd, New Rules!	9
3. What's in a Name?	17
4. Traveling Boots	27
5. Advanced Training	39
6. Skunks Galore!	45
7. Who's a Pony?	53
8. C.R.H.A. Adventures	61
9. SOS!	75
10. Shady Lady	81
11. Spotted Patrol	85
12 A Long Road Home	89
13. More Lazy Summer Days	93
Appendix.	--
Rangerbred Facts	97
Author Notes	100
Meet the Illustrator	104
Excerpt BYHT Sox	106
Excerpt Frosty and the Nightstalker	109

INTRODUCTION

I found a safe spot under a giant sycamore tree to doze in the warmth of the sun. My lifelong reputation had been passed down to the new generation of horses who now occupied the home I had come to love. My infamy played in my favor, and the youngsters pretty much kept their distance.

The late autumn rays filtered through the few remaining leaves, warming my back and old bones. I felt decades younger as I nodded off. Visions of Mom and my early life danced in my memory as I recalled how I had found my place in the world.

1
Lazy Summer Days

My memories zoomed in on the beginning of my life and how I became a backyard horse during my yearling summer. Until that fateful summer, I lived on a large horse farm not far from where I was to spend the formative years of my life. My mother was the boss mare, and while I was still a little filly nursing at her side, she told me. "Never let any of the other foals push you around. Timid horses don't fare as well as the more aggressive ones."

Momma was always first in line to enter the barn for the evening feed, and no one challenged her. As I became more aware of the hierarchy of herd life, I grew a little bolder and strayed farther from Mom's side. Under the guidance of my mother, her traits soon became mine. I heard whispers around the pasture that I did not understand. Curious, I asked Mom, "What does 'Plain Jane' mean?"

"Where did you hear that term, daughter?"

"The other foals said their moms call you and Toy 'Plain Janes."

"It is just sour apples. Little ones repeat whatever their parents say. Unfortunately, some of the other mares are jealous. Toy and I do not have Appaloosa coat patterns, but we both produce loud colored foals. Don't pay any attention to them."

"Well, I think you are the most beautiful of all the mares, Mom."

She nuzzled me. "Thank you dear. You're a lovely filly and will grow to be a real
beauty."

I didn't know about the beauty part, but I did have some spots the color of my mom's solid coat. She told me once the color was called "liver chestnut." I'd inherited the same star as Mom, smack in the middle of our foreheads, but mine was not as easily seen amid the spots that covered my face. No matter how hard I stared at my reflection in the pond or a water trough I could barely see it. My hind socks were also inherited from Mom, and they stood out well on my dark chestnut legs. Above my knees and hocks, I was white with multi-colored spots in various sizes. Some of my spots had what Mom referred to as a halo around them.

Toy was Mom's best friend. She'd been injured as a young horse, and the mishap left her blind in one eye. Mom, like a good friend, always stood on Toy's blind side to protect her. Toy was a buckskin, which is kind of a gold color with a black mane and tail. Her legs were black from her knees and hocks down. She also had a few random white spots on her golden coat. Her spots were about the size of a kernel of corn. Her daughter, Sugar, was born a couple of days after me, and we hung around together as foals and weanlings. Sugar was the name the humans gave to Toy's foal. My new friend was a true leopard, white from her nose to her hooves. She had large, quarter and half-dollar size, golden spots splashed about on her white coat. In the same way that some of my spots and the color of my legs matched my mom's coat, Sugar's spots were the color of Toy's coat.

Sugar thought that we were related because I had a few gold spots here and there in my coat too, along with some reddish chestnut spots. Actually, Sugar was pretty close with her relationship estimate. As our mothers explained the facts of life to us, it turned out that we were half-sisters. Now, the word from the older generation was that all of our sire's offspring had at least one red chestnut spot somewhere on their body. Some of the foals, like me, had several spots of that color on their hides. It became a game with us to locate the inherited spot on the other foals.

"Hey, Sugar, the only red spot I can find on you is on the back of your right ear."

Some of the famous marks were well hidden. We dodged a few kicks if we got too personal in our search.

"Watch out for Bertha and her friends." Sugar warned me. "They are a nasty bunch. It's a lot safer to check out the colts."

We tired of the game after a few days of attempting to catalog the hereditary spot on the rest of our pasture mates. Our new topic of conversation centered around the strange humans who showed up to gawk at us.

"Sugar, do you find it strange that the people tramping through our pasture and peeking into our stalls call us both leopards?"

Sugar thought about my observation before offering her viewpoint. "Though your dark legs keep you from being a true leopard, my mom says that you look enough like one to fool people."

"Could be your mom's poor eyesight, Sugar. My mom told me that leopards are white from head to hoof with spots on their coats, like you. Mom also said that some leopards have a lot of Appaloosa markings and others practically none at all."

The human population of the farm, as well as visitors, started calling me Love.

DON'T CALL ME LOVE

Like all the other foals, I sought out Mom to explain what I didn't understand. "Mom, what does Love mean?"

"Well, daughter, I overheard one of the grooms tell another that you were registered as Chelsea Love. So, the humans gave you Love as your barn name."

I had no idea what registered meant, but I filed it away in my memory banks. What I did know, was that I took a lot of teasing once word of my name got circulated to the other horses. The harassment about my name continued throughout the fall and winter. I guess that the other mothers thought I was misnamed. The constant teasing did not do my disposition any good. Fall arrived, and we were all put in a separate pasture from our mothers. I kicked and bit a few of the other weanlings butts when they repeated what their had mothers had told them.

Sugar went away with some unfamiliar humans before Christmas. We didn't even get to say goodbye! The colts were separated from us fillies in the spring. We had all grown a lot throughout the long year. I could see Mom with her new foal over in the adjoining pasture. My new sibling didn't look at all like me! The new foal had a big snowflake pattern on its rump, but otherwise was solid like our Mom, with the same star and hind socks. "Oh, my! Mom's new foal is a colt," I snorted. Toy had lost her foal a couple of months earlier, so my little brother had two overprotective mares to keep him in line and make sure he didn't get too adventurous too soon. He couldn't get away with anything.

No one much bothered me anymore; they knew better, but the little filly Blue was always picked on and excluded from the filly clique. I guess that when Sugar and I were growing up together we didn't pay much attention to the other foals, except to put an occasional upstart in their place. I never realized how small Blue was.

Blue, alone as usual, had found a yummy patch of clover not far from where I was grazing. The gang of four—the nasty girls that always made fun of my name—decided they wanted Blue's patch of clover.

"Scram, midget. You don't rate sweet clover."

Outnumbered, Blue started to back off. When she saw me coming at her from behind she froze. Bertha, the ringleader of the pack, was so occupied bullying Blue that she didn't notice me. She laid back her ears and scrunched up her nostrils, making an ugly face at Blue and then threatening her. "I told you to get lost, Blue, unless you want a beating!"

I whizzed past the frightened Blue, and took a chunk out of big mouth Bertha's spotted hide. Then, I whipped around and clocked her with a hind foot for good measure. One of her friends, Lotta, tried a rear attack. I let go with both hind legs and sent her flying off of her feet. The other two gang members were long gone. I laid my ears back and challenged them, "Come on! You want to try again? I am just getting warmed up." They backed off, and I turned my attention to Blue.

I had never noticed before, probably because she tried to stay out of everyone's way, but Blue was very pretty with her black coat and white snowflakes. I told her, "Eat your clover, Blue. They won't be back."

"Thank you, Love! Would you share the patch of sweet clover with me? I am sure there is enough for two."

After that day, Blue became my new pasture buddy. A few weeks later, the gang of four became the gang of three. By the end of the month the humans call June, they had become the gang of two. It was funny, or maybe not, but as their numbers dwindled, so did their bullying. Another four weeks passed and a family of humans took Blue with them. I left the farm of my birth a few days after my new little friend. I wondered if I would ever see my mother and my little brother again or my friends Sugar and Blue.

I was very reluctant to leave everyone that I knew and all that was familiar to me. My new humans were persistent. From the beginning, it required all their patience to convince me to step into the metal box on wheels. I'd watched other horses go into the trailer trap, from the safety of my pasture, and they all disappeared never to be seen again. I didn't know where they went, but I didn't want to disappear like the others. I thought they might give up and go away if I held my ground.

2
New Herd, New Rules

The short ride to my new home had been frightening. I recall how the humans had tricked me with a bucket of the yummy sweet feed I have always loved. I took a couple of mouthfuls, and then they took it away to sprinkle some on the floor of the scary trap. My hunger for the molasses-coated grain defeated my resolve. As I reached farther into the trailer to nibble at the oats and pellets, I made the mistake of hopping in to reach more of the tasty offering. The metal stall on wheels shook and wiggled when my hooves hit the rubber-covered floor. Then wham! The doors closed behind me with a loud noise that echoed around the metal trap, and scared the poop right out of me. I forgot all about the grain that I was busy grinding beneath my scrambling hooves.

The whole experience would have been a lot more traumatic if the human named Terrie hadn't ridden in the trailer with me on that first fateful trip. She understood that I was terrified when the stall began to move. "Oh. Great Horse in heaven please save me!" I prayed. My human companion reassured me by stroking my neck and talking to me in a soft voice, *"Easy, Love, you will find your balance soon. We are almost home."*

At that time, I was not good at understanding the human language and not very adept translating the static sound they spoke. Most of their words came out as blah, blah, blah, but I remember thinking that my home was somewhere behind me along with my mom and little brother. I took the measure of this young woman. Her hair was a lighter shade of gold than what Toy's coat had been, and she had eyes the color of the summer sky. She looked kind of skinny to me, but it was hard for me to judge; I didn't know many humans.

My companion was right the bumpy ride was soon over. The metal stall stopped moving, and the door behind me opened once more. Terrie pushed on my chest and told me to *"back up."* Okay, time out! I didn't have a clue what she was yakking about, so she repeated the words and poked me in the chest again. I took a step back, and she stopped jabbing at my chest to praise me. *"Good girl, Love.* Cautiously, I took a couple of more steps back, and suddenly my back foot slipped out into midair. I quickly brought it back in with my other feet.

It took me a couple of false starts and a lot of work on Terrie's part to get me out of that thing. Once I got both hind feet back on solid ground, my front end was out of there in a flash. I thanked the great horse gods for getting me out of the frightening ride in one piece. Toy always told Sugar and me that if we were good fillies, the great horse in heaven would look out for us. My mom used to snort at her friend's comment. I'm not sure whether Mom didn't believe in the horse spirits, or if she figured I couldn't be good long enough to qualify for their divine protection.

All the strange voices nickering at me made me a bit nervous, but I tagged along with Terrie to my new stall. My new place was clean and comfortable, but I paced its confines while listening intently to the strange new voices. I noticed that all the other occupants were adults when Terrie and I first strolled up the aisle of what she referred to as my *new home*. The only grown up horses I had any experience with were limited to my mom and the other broodmares I had been with since the day I was born.

On my second day, I was turned out alone in a small paddock. Terrie groomed me in the morning and talked to me, but I only understood a few words. *"You can spend most of the day in the riding arena, Love. You'll be close to the other horses, but separated until you become acquainted with them."*

I watched the four older horses from the safety of my isolated turnout area. The riding arena at my new home was a far cry from the huge pastures where I had spent the first year of my life. The only grass was at the edges of the fence lines. The adults ran around the larger paddock bucking, rearing, and playing tag. I raised my tail so high that it curled over my back, as I snorted, shook my head, and whizzed around my playpen.

It didn't take long for the other horses to calm down. I figured that's how it was with older horses. Soon, the adult residents of that little farm were busy munching grass. I continued to run around and kick up my heels for a while longer before I was ready to settle down.

I grazed my way around the pen eating the sparse grass along the fence. I was distracted from the pursuit of tasty green morsels by the approach of two horses. An intriguing patch of clover had briefly sidetracked one of them: both were mares as I recall. The tall black mare with a high head carriage leaned over the fence and said, "Hello." She sounded friendly, so I wandered over to talk with her. As I approached, she told me her name. "My name is Kid-O. What is your name?"

I moved closer and cautiously touched noses with her as I answered her question. "I'm called Love." Kid-O didn't know me yet, so she was unable to comment on the irony of my name.

She just laughed and said, "Humans sure pick funny names for us. My first owner was a doctor, and he named me Caduceus Heather, but my new owner hated it. He started to call me Kid-O because I was the youngest when I first came here."

Curios, I asked her, "How old were you?"

"I was about your age, I guess. I was barely past my first birthday when I arrived, and that was three years ago, by the humans' calendar."

"And you are the youngest?" I thought the others must be really old!

"Yep, and as the only Morgan I am outnumbered by stock horses."

"What is a stock horse?" I asked her. It was a new term for me. Kid-O laughed and looked over her shoulder at the others. "You and everyone else on this farm have ranch horses in their heritage, and you will most likely become a western horse."

We paused in our conversation to watch the approach of a blood bay mare with a huge white blanket decorated with a zillion bay haloed spots. She had no face markings or white on her black legs. Her black mane and tail ruffled in the mild breeze.

Kid-O introduced us. "Millie, this is Love, the newest member of our herd."

The pretty bay Appaloosa mare looked me over, and then she touched noses with me. "Do you have a registered name, Love?"

"My mother told me that my registered name is Chelsea Love." I said in a disgusted tone of voice that must have sounded like I hated my name. The bay mare picked up on my attitude in a flash.

"Well, it could be worse. Look at the name Kid-O has to show under. My registered name is Chilly Millie, and I get my share of bad jokes about it from the boys in our group."

Both mares moved over a little to make room for a dapple-gray gelding who had been close enough to overhear the conversation we girls were having. He was bigger than Millie who was not much taller than me, but twice my width. Kid-O still had a couple of inches on him at the withers although she appeared much taller due to her high headset.

He looked me over much the same way Millie had; the difference was the devilish look in his eyes. I had absolutely zero experience with grown male horses, but I remembered how rough the colts were before we were separated as yearlings.

"Hello, little Spots. I'm Cutter. You're a pretty little filly. When do you suppose you will be able to come out to keep us company?"

I wasn't sure if he was being friendly or trying to test my temper. Either way, I set him straight. "My name isn't Spots: it is Chelsea Love! While I don't really like my name, it beats the heck out of being called spots." I laid my ears back and snorted at him for emphasis.

Cutter laughed at my display of temper. He then told me something that I would remember for the rest of my life. "My name isn't really Cutter. It was a name my original owner gave me after our first season of Cutting Horse competitions. He'd told me, 'You have earned a better name than Squeaky."

That had been a bit of a shock, and I tried not to laugh. This large muscular guy with an obviously masculine voice couldn't have such a silly name, so I asked for clarification on the name and the cutting thing. "What is a cutting horse?"

"A cutting horse works with cattle, moving them from one place to another. Sometimes, we have to separate cows, calves, or steers from the herd to be branded or doctored. However, in competitions, we are judged on how quietly we go into the herd, separate the calf our rider selects and our ability to keep that critter from returning to the herd. We can work up to three calves in the time allotted."

I really didn't know much more than before I'd asked him. It might have made more sense if I had a clue what a cow was, but I didn't want to appear ignorant as well as young; so I nodded my head like I knew exactly what he was telling me.

"Someday, you may be able to earn a name you like better than Love. See y'all later. Bye, little one." Then he turned away to join a larger dark horse in the pasture.

Millie whispered to me "I told you your name could be worse. As a baby Cutter was named Big Boy's Squeaky Toy."

The three of us giggled at the strange name that had been given to him as a young foal. When the others wandered back to their grazing I decided that Chelsea Love wasn't so bad after all. Still, a cool nickname would be super.

The following day went much like the one before, except I had to splay my legs more widely while turning my head to the side and stretching my neck to reach the taller grass on the other side of my fenced in enclosure. My three new friends stopped by in the afternoon to say hello and chat. Then they abruptly turned away to make room for the huge dark horse. I had seen this behavior before. Like my mother in the broodmare band—here was the boss horse. He was as tall as Kid-O, but twice as wide as the slim mare. Muscles bulged under his dark coat, and a white star sat dead center of his forehead. His pink muzzle looked like a child had splattered black paint on it with a watercolor brush. His coat sparkled with a dark chocolate color that had black spots scattered throughout it. The only white on him other than the star on his head was a small sock on one hind leg and snowflakes across his rump. His mane and tail were black.

The size of him, and his obvious strength were a bit intimidating, but his eyes were kind. I had expected him to sound like Cutter with a strong male voice, but when he spoke his voice was much deeper, like the rumble of thunder. I admit that the first time I heard his voice it unnerved me.

"The others tell me that you're named Chelsea Love. Is that correct?"

I heard my mother's voice in my head, "Don't let anyone push you around, daughter." I tried to draw on the strength she had instilled in me before I answered him. "Yeah, that's the name I was given. What of it?" Okay, that came out a little bratty and antagonistic. He didn't seem to take any offense with my hostile response to his question. However, he looked at me like I was a bug that he could squash whenever he chose.

He picked up the questioning again. "Do you know your father's name?"

"My mother told me my sire's name is Chief Chelsea." I tried to be a little more polite this time. Mom always said to be polite to the older mares even if I didn't like them. I figured that was good advice with all older horses.

"Well then, it looks like you're my little sister. Chelsea is also my sire," he told me.

Sometimes the devil gets the better of me. I responded belligerently, "No. That only makes us a half-brother and sister. I'm sure you're much older than my mother."

He gave me that insignificant bug look again, turned his big frosted butt to me, and walked away without another word.

"Hey, old guy! What's your name?" I yelled after him.

He turned only long enough to grace me with a response. "They call me Frosty."

"Is that all? Just Frosty?" He didn't bother to answer me. To him I didn't matter. I was at the bottom of the pecking order, and he was at the top. The problems at my new home arose because I was used to being at the top while at my mother's side. I held my rank as a yearling, and I had absolutely zero intention of languishing at the bottom of the social ladder for long.

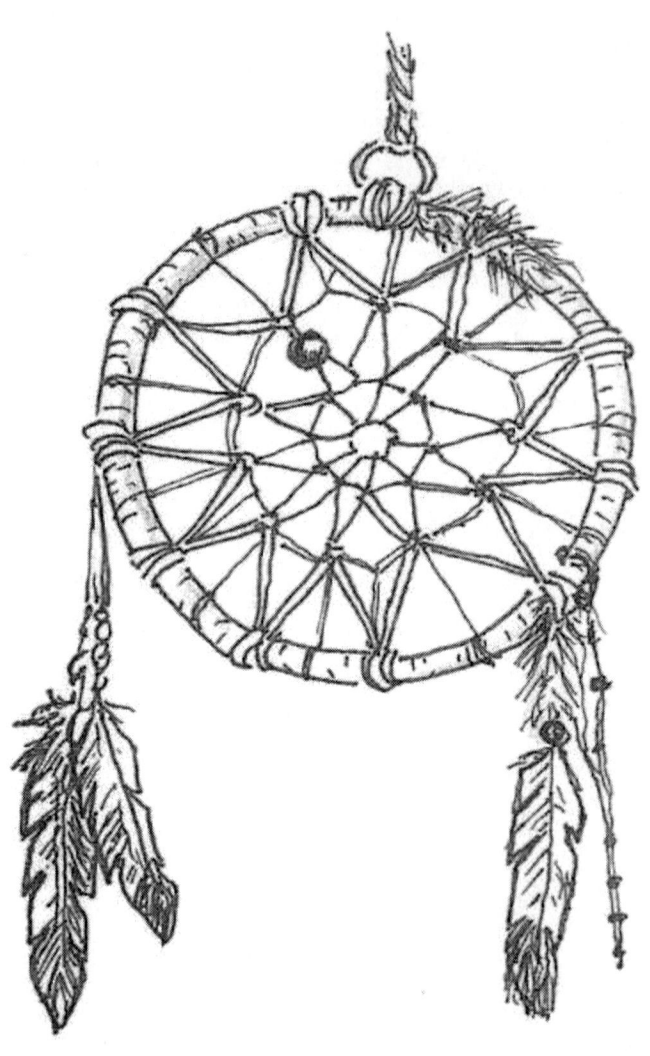

3
What's in a Name?

I spent the next four days in the small arena behind the barn. Early mornings, Terrie came out to groom me, and then she would leave. Marcie, who had been there when Terrie picked me up a week earlier, put me out behind the barn as soon as she completed whatever she was doing with the boss horse. Marcie was shorter than Terrie and quite a bit rounder. It was hard to tell what color her eyes were. They seemed to change with her mood, or perhaps with the weather. Sometimes they were gray, other times they looked green with a yellow ring around the pupil, and once in a while they almost mirrored Terrie's. Marcie's hair was almost as dark as Frosty's coat. Each morning, she climbed onto his back to ride him around in the area where I was usually turned out. That made one more black mark on the dislike list that I had filed in my head. I couldn't go out until Marcie finished with him. Truthfully, I didn't have anything on a like list for my half-brother.

Whenever she finally finished with him, she led me to the small enclosure I had been occupying since I arrived. Then she took the others out. Frosty was put out last, and I noticed the first thing he did was pick the big dusty spot not far from the gate to roll. I filed away the turn out order and the habits of the older horses.

On what Kid-O told me was a weekend, things changed. Terrie stayed to help with the turnouts. She put me out dead last. Marcie worked the gate while Terrie took me out back with the adult horses for the first time. I pranced beside her in my excitement. The only drawback to the whole issue of joining the others was the big boss horse and how to deal with him. Terrie turned me loose, and I made a beeline for the bare patch of ground where Frosty was busy rolling. I kicked him in the butt twice while he was down and then ran like heck! I heard Terrie and Marcie groan as I clocked him, and the other horses all stopped their grazing to watch me get creamed. Instead of coming after me, Frosty got up, shook off the excess dirt, walked over to the water trough to take a drink, and then went under a big sycamore tree to munch some grass in the shade.

I kept an eye on him for most of the day. I figured sooner or later he would come over and thump me. However, it was Millie's reaction that undid me.

She turned her back on me and gave me the cold shoulder. I complained to Kid-O. "I thought we were friends. Now she won't even look at me!"

"Frosty is our protector, and Millie loves him the most. She was born here, and when she was weaned she was turned out with Frosty. Mostly he only tolerated the little weanling, less than six months old, but he kept an eye on her. One day, a couple of large dogs came after Millie. She told me she whinnied in fright and ran to find Frosty. He was already on his way, and she ran behind him. He picked up the closest dog by the fur on its back and flung it across the paddock. While he was occupied with the first dog, the second one decided on a rear attack going for Frosty's, back legs, a big mistake. He sent that one flying through the air with a well-placed kick. Millie said that the dogs took off for home and safety. He has driven off coyotes, and countless stray dogs."

I hated lectures, even when I knew I deserved one. "I'm not afraid of dogs. I can take care of myself." My boast was more to reassure myself than it was bragging. I didn't even know what a dog was. Cats roamed the barn and pastures where I was raised, and I saw a few here. But, like the cows Cutter had tried to explain to me, I was as clueless about dogs and coyotes. Kid-O continued her praises of my half-brother.

"We've had some rowdy colts join our herd over the years. Frosty was always quick to protect us and to put the offender in his place. Once or twice, he had larger colts try to challenge him, but he made quick work of knocking them down a peg or two. Lucky that you're a filly and his little sister, or you would be in a world of hurt by now."

I have to admit that I was a bit embarrassed about what the others considered to be my sneak attack on their leader. The following week went pretty much the same. Millie still wasn't talking to me, Frosty and Cutter ignored me, and only Kid-O spent time with me. You would think I had something contagious the way they all acted. I wondered how long they could stay mad at me. What a bummer!

Then the rains came. Not soft, easy showers, but big thunderstorms. Three days of constant rain! The peaceful trickling river on the other side of our back pasture fence overflowed, and the floodwaters knocked down trees that, in turn, got caught in our fences and took them down.
The sun returned on the fourth day of our confinement. That day we watched as Terrie, Marcie, and her husband, George, worked on repairing our fences.

I was going stir-crazy, and I wanted to scream, "LET ME OUT!!!" I bucked and reared in my stall.

Whenever the humans came out to feed us or to do other chores, I pounded on my door with a well-placed hoof. They didn't seem to get the message. The fence repair crew worked almost two days before we were able to go out again. It was on that glorious day I managed to get myself on the bad side of George. When Kid-O had told me that George was Marcie's husband, she'd also filled me in that he was Terrie's brother. I have to admit she was a lot more respectful of her big brother than I was of mine. George towered over his wife and sister. Marcie's head barely reached his chin. Terrie had a couple of more inches on Marcie. George and his sister had a strong family resemblance. Both of them possessed flaxen manes and sky blue eyes. Easygoing and kind of laid back, it took a lot to get George upset, but I managed to do it without even trying.

Looking back on that day, I know that turnouts went quicker than normal with three people helping out, but it felt like an eternity to me. I was ready to explode when—dead last—my turn finally came. The other horses were having a gallop around the pasture, and I danced around on my lead rope as Terrie took me out to the gate. George opened the gate for me, and as soon as Terrie unhooked the snap from my halter, I took off.

I ran down the front fence line that separated the back pasture from the deep sand work arena where I had spent my first four days. I shook my head and kicked out. Bam! The middle fence board popped off. That was kind of fun, so I took aim at the next one. Wham! Bang! Crack! I kicked down three boards and shattered one. I was pretty proud of myself. On a dead run I hadn't miss one time! My high didn't last too long though. George's string of angry words singed my innocent young ears from all the way across the pasture, and I knew that he didn't appreciate my marksmanship.

"Hey, Dead Eye, I wouldn't be surprised if you got your spotted butt sold after all that destruction." As usual, I didn't know whether Cutter was teasing me or he was being serious. I wondered if Terrie would get rid of me because I had broken the fence.

Daily life went more smoothly the following month or so, and my energy level was more manageable.

Terrie had begun to teach me how to work on a lunge-line. I circled her on one end of the long line while she held the other end. She urged me on with her voice and a long whip that made a loud popping sound near my hind end. I also learned to stand up correctly when she led me around. She called that work routine "halter and showmanship training." I was required to trot beside her, stop with my feet square, and not move. I heard Marcie warn her when she would pick up one of my hind feet to place it where she wanted it. *"Be careful Terrie! That horse is quick with those rear guns."* Once more I was confused. I didn't know what Marcie meant by rear guns, but I had a feeling it wasn't a good thing.

The commands to walk, trot, and canter on the lunge weren't hard for me, and I learned quickly. Whoa, gave me more trouble, especially on the days Terrie tried to work me in the mornings before I got to go out and play. It was way too much for me to handle a stop when she commanded me to whoa. I was still a youngster, at the time, and my attention span had been very short. I got bored quickly. Terrie pretty much gave up on my halter training during the morning. She started coming for a little while in the evening after I got the running and bucking out of my system. I really liked all the attention, and I tried to learn my lessons.

Millie talked to me sometimes, but she wasn't friendly. Kid-O and Cutter were the ones who talked to me, ran, played, and grazed with me. Millie spent most of her time with Frosty. As for my big half-brother, he hadn't talked to me since my sneak attack. He sure could hold a grudge! He didn't look at me like I was a bug anymore, but he acted as if I were invisible. Maybe he was getting old and couldn't see well any more. I shared my conclusion about Frosty's vision with Kid-O. She told me, "Frosty isn't that old. He is only twelve by human calculations." I processed that information and the rest of what she told me. "We age differently than our humans. You're one year old, but you are equivalent to a human child of four. I'm a horse of four and equal to a sixteen-year-old human."

I asked her, "If my brother is twelve, how many human years does he equal?"

"I don't know, Love. My math skills aren't very good, but some horses live a long time. Cutter could probably tell you more. He told me once that his sire had been almost forty when he went to sleep in a sunny pasture and never woke up."

I was not inclined to ask Cutter anything that would allow him to spin another tall tale. He sure could tell some whoppers!

Summer was ending, and I was introduced to the treat of apples. George and Marcie cleaned up most of the yummy fruit before we could go out, and I wondered what they did with them. In addition to the humans stealing our apples, the deer liked them, too. Large deer and little fawns with white spots on their backs gathered under a big apple tree outside the furthest fence line of our pasture. I had a hunch that when we were in the barn they probably munched up our apples, too.

I remember well the events of the second week in month in where trees began to change the color of their leaves. The deer, like us, were browsing for the few remaining apples that had hit the ground. I'd noticed the tall grass on our side of the river started to sway, but there was not even a breeze that morning! The deer perked their ears up, and in a flash they were on a dead run away from the river, the fawns ran right on the heels of their mothers who had sensed danger. Three brown furry creatures bounded out of the tall swaying grass, and were hot on the deer's trail, but the deer were too quick. So the funny furry creatures turned their attention to us.

Cutter and Kid-O had gone on a trial ride earlier that morning, right after breakfast. That left me with cold-shoulder Millie and my-not-so friendly brother. Following the deer escape, the four-legged hunters returned to try us on for size. Millie took one look and hightailed it to the front of the pasture. I was a little slower to take flight, for I had been trying to figure out exactly what they were. Then I heard Millie yell. "Coyotes in the pasture!"

By the time she had called out the warning, it was too late to run. The three of them had zeroed in on me, and I wasn't going to turn my back on them. I pinned my ears back, and scrunched up my nose, in what I hoped was as ugly a face as Bertha used to make. I attempted to show them I was not a helpless deer. I guess my face wasn't ugly enough to intimidate them. They had moved from a cautious stalking mode to a full-out attack. The trio of coyotes had picked up speed and were intent on taking me down when my huge brother barreled into the center of them and bellowed at me.

"Run, little dummy!"

It wasn't that I had been unhappy to see him. His arrival surely evened up the odds, but it made me mad that he called me a dummy, and I'd never been inclined to turn tail and run from a fight. He stomped one coyote, but the other two were headed my way. The frontal assault had cost the life of one of them, so they tried to take me down from behind. "Big mistake, fur ball!" I hollered in my most intimidating young voice, and sent one of them airborne with a good swift kick. I clocked it. The critter yelped and hit the ground running for the tall grass on the other side of our pasture fence, followed closely by the uninjured member of the small pack. I was feeling pretty proud of myself. Then the lecture came.

"Are you crazy, little sister? Don't you know they were planning to have you for lunch? You need to be more aware of what is going on around you!"

I was not going to admit that he had probably saved me, but good manners meant I should, at least, thank him for his help. "Well, thank you for the heroics, but I could have handled them."

It was a lie, and he knew it. He didn't say a word; he simply turned his back on me and went over to make sure the coyote he had stomped on was dead. I wondered what he would do if it was still alive. Fortunately, I didn't have to find out. The nasty little creature was now in the Happy Hunting Grounds of his ancestors.

Marcie had heard the ruckus and arrived as I'd launched one of the coyotes into the air. She removed the carcass from our pasture and then checked each of us.

"What is she looking for?" I questioned my brother.

"Marcie is looking for any bite marks."

Millie still didn't talk much to me, but she sure blabbed about the coyote attack the next day when Kid-O and Cutter joined us in the pasture. Kid-O thought I had been very brave, but Cutter, like Frosty, thought I was crazy and darned lucky. Man, those old guys didn't want to give a girl any credit!

We were favored with a warm spell the following week. We all had our last baths before winter set in. Baths always made me itchy, and I would get this uncontrollable urge to roll on the ground or in my stall. That morning Terrie hosed me off then tied me in my stall to dry. As usual, I was the last one turned out, but I was now the first to come in at feeding time. I trotted over to Frosty's favorite spot and plunked down for a long overdue roll in the sandy soil. I got up, shook off the extra dirt, let out a couple of bucks, and started to lope out near the rest of the herd. Out of nowhere, a smaller version of the coyote darted under the fence to chase me. I popped it one and sent it rolling in the dirt. It cried something pitiful. When I turned to check it out, Marcie chased me away with a whip, while Terrie with water running from her eyes, picked up the small critter and cradled it in her arms.

I wandered out back, puzzled by the by the two human's reactions. Marcie wasn't upset about the dead or injured coyotes, but she angrily chased me away from this one. Kid-O approached. "Love, what did you do?" That was Terrie's little Beagle dog you just brained!"

So, that was a dog! It was all very confusing to me. Apparently it was okay to stomp or kick a coyote, but not a dog. How the heck was I supposed to tell the difference? Frosty scolded me and told me the coyotes wanted to make a meal out of me. Then, Kid-O said the little dog only wanted to play and for me not to be surprised if Terrie found another horse.

Frosty saw my confusion, and actually talked to me! "Don't be too upset Love. You're very young, and while you must be aware of what is around you, it's important to develop a sense of a threat. You need to figure out what is a danger and what isn't. Pay attention, little sister, and you'll learn to tell the difference, as you grow older. One hint, Love, never kick a human. That'll get you out of here quicker than anything else."

Fortunately, for me, the little dog survived. I could sense that Terrie was upset with me. George and Marcie stopped calling me Love and renamed me Gunny. Soon, the other horses picked up on my new moniker. Cutter thought my new name fit me better than Love.

After that fall, I seldom heard my registered name again, except on the public address systems when it was announced at a horse show. I'd earned my new name as a yearling, and it stuck for the rest of my life.

JACKIE ANTON

4
Traveling Boots

All the breakfasts in the horse trailer my yearling year finally made sense. I hadn't been enthused about getting in noisy metal trap again. I worried my aggressive nature was going to get me shipped down the road. Marcie put Kid-O in the trailer in the beginning to reassure me. By that fall, I was loading and unloading like an old pro. We even went for a couple of short rides, but we always came back home. As a result I stopped worrying that getting into the trailer meant I was going to lose my second home.

My first horse show was in May of my two-year-old year. Terrie always wrapped my legs whenever I went into the trailer. The wraps were long blue stretchy cloth strips that wound around my legs and fastened with sticky strips that she called "Velcro." The wraps padded my legs from slightly below my knees and hocks to my ankles. Frosty and Millie went on that first show trip with me and it had been the longest ride of my life, at that time. We bounced and swayed down the road for only two hours, according to Terrie. To me, the trip felt like forever so I kept asking. "Are we there yet?" Frosty groaned as if he were in pain, when I asked the same question five or six more times.

Finally, he lowered himself to answer me. "You will know when we get to the show. There will be many horse trailers and a lot of other horses."

I filed his response in my expanding database of knowledge. Our destination sounded exciting! I waited for what seemed like an eternity before I asked again "Are we there yet?"

That time in addition to my brother's disgusted sigh, Millie hollered at me. "SHUT UP! Just eat your hay."

She was riding in the front of the four-horse trailer next to Frosty, who had the left hand stall. I really couldn't see them from my position behind my grouchy brother. Occasionally, I caught a glimpse of a wrapped hind leg. I occupied the stall behind Frosty and was the only horse in the rear set of stalls. Most of my time was spent gawking at the strange world as it whizzed by. I was about to risk asking again when the trailer slowed down. We all braced as our ride made a wide turn. I peeked out the side window and saw more trailers than I could count. A virtual rainbow of colors filled the whole parking area in front of two long barns. I trembled with anticipation at the sight of so many other horses.

When we were unloaded I went first. As I stepped out of the trailer, I gazed at what appeared to be all the Appaloosa horses in the world

Excited, I called out. "Hello! I am Chelsea Love. Is there anyone out there that I know?" I perked my ears up when Sugar answered my call. It surprised me to hear a colt also answer me.

"Hey, Love, it's me, Patch, your brother!" His voice sounded older, but still familiar. I tried to remember what his registered name was. It wasn't until the next morning when they announced the winner of the yearling stallion class that it came back to me. My little brother's name was Chelsea's Patch O Snow. Not only did he win his age class, but he also won the junior stallion championship at halter.

As it turned out, Sugar and I were in the same halter class. She won, and I came in second in the two-year-old filly class. Terrie also entered me in the most colorful class. That is where I won my very first blue ribbon and trophy.

After my halter classes, I followed Terry into the first of the large barns to rest while Frosty and Millie showed in riding classes. Whatever those were. I sure had a lot to learn about horse shows.

I did so well on my first outing that Terrie gave me a new bright red pair of shipping boots and a matching red halter. The shipping boots took some getting used to. Opened they looked like a big square of red nylon on the outside, with fuzzy black padding on the inside that touched my skin. The new wraps covered my legs all the way down to my hooves and closed with four Velcro strips. The Velcro fasteners on each of the wraps made them fit snugly. They felt strange, bulkier than what I was used to, and I tried to kick them off of my back legs, but they held fast. Terrie lunged me for several days wearing the boots until I got used to them.

Frosty joked, "You should wear those red traveling boots in the next most colorful class competition; you would be a sure winner." For once in my life, I was speechless. I'd never heard him make a wisecrack. In fact, I didn't think he had a sense of humor.

The previous fall I'd been introduced to wide leather girth, known as a surcingle, that fit around my back and belly. Brass rings were attached to the top and sides of it. An English saddle was put on my back over the winter months. Sometimes Terrie would attach long lines through the rings of the surcingle or the saddle and walk behind me. She called that routine "ground driving." When it was too icy or stormy outdoors she guided me up and down the aisle of our barn. Cutter had a good time heckling me. "Straighten up, Love. You're weaving like a horse on loco weed!" I didn't back straight enough to suit him either. My turns were another area of criticism. "Great Horse in heaven, Love, do you need ten acres to change direction? Tighten up those turnarounds!"

Terrie and I were confined to the barn for almost a week, and Cutter was really getting to me. No one, including him had called me Love for months, and the sarcastic way he said it stoked my temper. The day he broke my effort to control my rising ire, Terrie had taken the small saddle to the tack room while I remained on the crossties in front of Cutter's stall. He was still heckling me, so I swung my butt around as far as I could and blasted his door while yelling at the top of my lungs, "DON'T CALL ME LOVE, you mangy cow chaser!"

Well, that display of temper got me scolded by Terrie, and cussed at by George who had to fix the front of Cutter's door. Cutter gave me a big horselaugh. Marcie threatened to evict me, and Terrie said, *"You'd better watch that kicking and destroying things. I don't think you would like a boarding stable should George and Marcie decide you're too dangerous to have around here."* I didn't have a clue what "evict" meant or what a boarding stable was, but neither sounded good the way the humans in my life spat those strange words at me. I knew I was in trouble and wanted to yell, "It was Cutter's fault. He made me do it!"

Oh well, I had survived the winter and early spring. My first horse show was under my belt, and I was comfortable with my shipping boots. It is a good thing that Terrie decided to spring the next lesson on me after I had been out most of the day. She groomed me like always, ending with picking out my hooves, and then she put the headstall with the O-ring snaffle on me. I still mouthed the bit some, but I was pretty okay with the feel of it by that time. Next she placed a saddle pad on me. That pad had been much larger and heavier than the one to which I'd become accustomed, but I hadn't been overly concerned.

WOW! Is she kidding me? She plunked a saddle on my back that weighed a ton! At least it felt that way to me. I'd seen Frosty and Cutter work with larger versions of what the humans called a western saddle, or sometimes they referred to it as a stock saddle. I snorted when Terrie placed it on my back. Then I heard Cutter making strange clucking noises. "What is the matter with you, cow brains?" I asked him.

Cutter wasn't the one who answered me; it was Kid-O who explained his taunt. "He's cheating with the chicken noises. He has a bet going with Frosty on how long it will take you to explode and make more trouble for Terrie."

I dug down deep into the well of inner strength that my parents had given me and stood like a giant oak. I had been every bit as rigid as the big tree in our back pasture, and I was afraid to move. Terrie removed the offensive object mere moments before my short fuse reached its end, and I blew up. I could breathe again and let out a huge sigh of relief, much to the amusement of the older horses.

A replay of the whole process went on for a couple of days before Terrie advanced me to working on the lunge-line with the saddle in place and the girth tightened up. I got a short reprieve from my new saddle when we left for my second horse show on Friday evening. That trip was only about half the distance of what the first one had been.

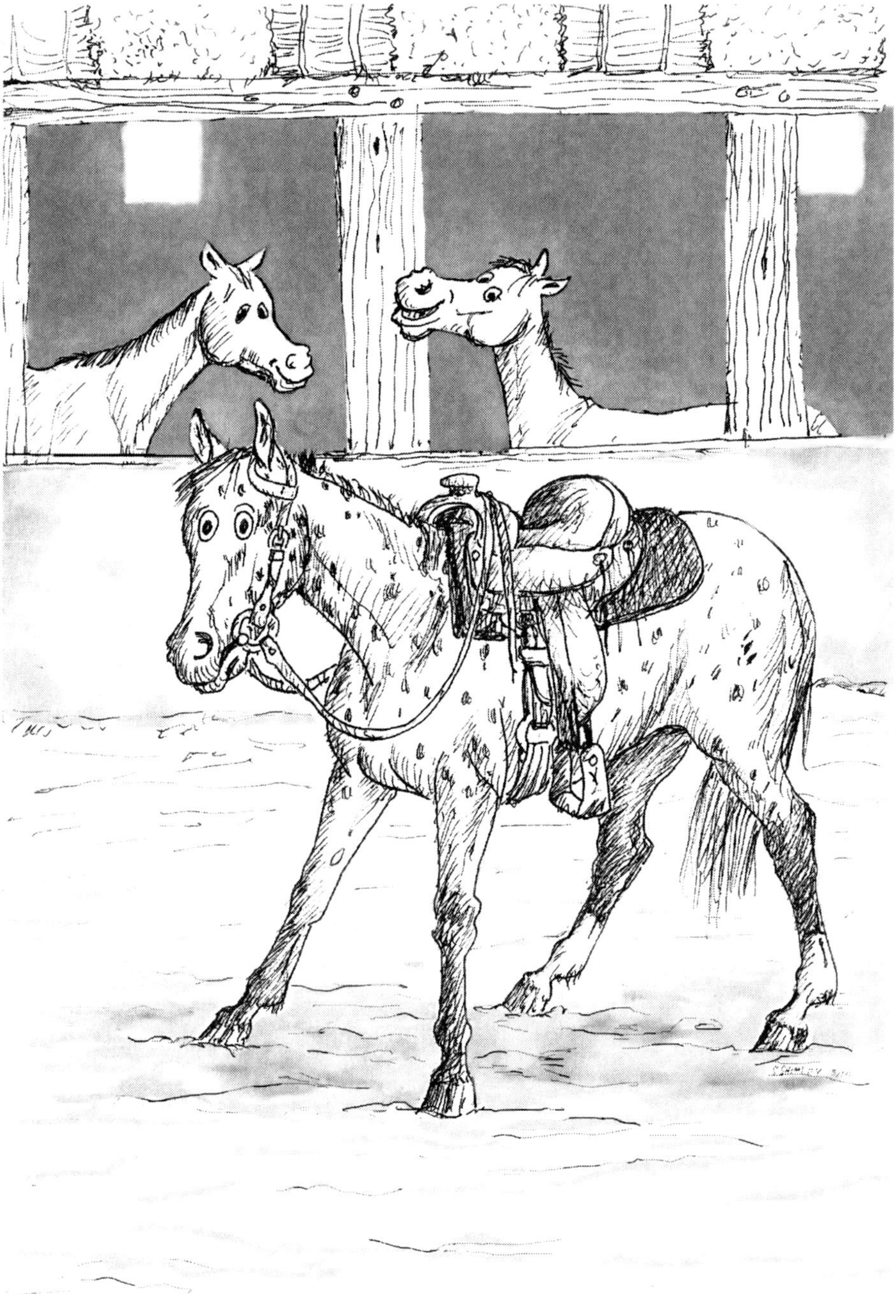

Once again, as I stepped from the trailer, I called out announcing my arrival, but no one answered me. Well, that wasn't entirely true. *"Darn it, Gunny, you hollered right in my ear! Do you have to bellow like that every time you get out of the trailer?"* Terrie complained as she gave my lead a little tug. She took me into the larger of the two barns that were visible to me. The barn that we entered actually had two stall rows that faced each other across a covered arena. The third barn stood separate. There weren't many horses there yet. Terrie and Marcie fed us, filled our water buckets, and gave us some hay.

George, according to Frosty, had gone to make entries for the show tomorrow and had taken the children with him. Kelly was seven years old, and Kara was four. Marcie's little girl was only two years older than me; she also had a knack for getting into trouble. Our humans left us in our stalls, and while we nibbled at our hay bags they went to feed the children.

Other horses began to arrive and fill in the empty stalls. When the children returned, they were put on the other two horses. Frosty carried little Kara. I watched Millie and Kelly as they walked and trotted around the arena with all the other youngsters who were practicing. Kelly was like looking at a younger version of his father, George. Frosty and tiny Kara, who resembled Marcie, circled on the end of the long line that was held by her mother. I wondered if Kara got dizzy as she went around and around on the lunge. Frosty just walked around Marcie while she talked to Kara. I didn't understand the things her mother was telling her, like how to sit and how to hold the reins.

Terrie decided to lunge me, in the middle of all the chaos. I did have a smidgen of trouble concentrating on her commands. I was busy trying to take it all in. The children were taken back to the strange looking little house that sat on the back of the blue truck. Our humans all disappeared after our work session.

33

It was dark on the other side of the large entry door by the time Terrie and Marcie returned, but the arena was well lit. Terrie passed me by and chose Millie. She occupied the stall between Frosty and me. I watched as they took the others outside. Where were they going in the dark? Were they leaving me behind because I had messed up on my commands earlier? I called out to them, but they didn't answer me.

I was about to call out again when Sugar walked in. I shifted my attention to my friend. The great Horse Spirit was with us. She was placed in the stall right next to me. Sugar greeted me. "Howdy, Love, I missed you at the last show."

Her greeting surprised me. "There were other shows since the last time we met?"

"It seems like there are shows every weekend," she sighed in a disgusted way.

"Don't you like horse shows, Sugar?" I asked my old friend. That's when I found out that she had been showing since she'd left our old home as a weanling filly. Though she was the same age as me, this was her third season of showing. She had been highpoint horse in her age division in three Appaloosa regional clubs as a weanling and yearling. It came as a shock to me that while I had been playing and munching grass at our old home Sugar had already been working. She'd spent a lot of time walking on something called a treadmill.

She explained it to me. "My new home has a narrow stall like contraption that they'd put me on when I was a little filly. The past year I've spent even more time on the raised rubber floor. A horse has to walk or trot depending on how fast the fake hill moves under their hooves."

"Why didn't you just get off of it?" I asked. It sounded terrible to me. I would have tried to escape.

"Once on it, you're enclosed on all sides, and your head is cross-tied. I was not subjected to it as much once I started working under saddle with the resident trainer at my new home."

That conversation with Sugar made me realize how good I had it at home with Terrie. My friend had five halter futurities under her belt, but she didn't seem happy.

That Saturday morning Patch repeated his wins of my first show, back in May, where we'd first been reunited. That same day, Sugar and I reversed positions I won our halter class, and she came in second. Our places qualified us for the junior mare champion class. There were six of us in the class. First and second place mares from the weanling, yearling, two-year-old, and three-year-old classes were eligible, but no weanlings showed up. Terrie was ecstatic that I stood champion junior mare. I know she would have been as thrilled if I had only made reserve champion, but Sugar's trainer was not pleased. He took her out of the ring then yanked on the chain of her show halter and made her work some more. He became the first human I really wanted to bite or kick.

I also won the most colorful class again. Terrie proudly hung my ribbons on the wire in the tack stall on the other side of Frosty, but she took my trophies with her. I relaxed, munched on my hay, and took in all the activity. It was quite a while later when Sugar returned to her stall. She was upset and didn't understand what she had done to be disciplined so harshly. I wasn't much help at making her feel better. I was as confused as my friend. From where I stood she did a bang-up job.

Kara and Frosty snagged a third place in lead line. Only children eight and under were eligible to enter that class where they were led by an adult, or an older child. I knew how the class worked because Frosty lowered himself enough to explain it to me. Kelly and Millie won the walk-trot class for children ten and under. Okay, I was confused. Frosty came to my rescue once more. "Children can't enter both classes, only one or the other. It all depends on their skill level. Kelly has been riding three years longer that his sister, and is able to guide Millie around at a walk and trot very well.

Frosty and Millie were saddled and bridled following an announced lunch break in the show. To my surprise so was Sugar. They all left me, Marcie and Frosty along with George and Millie. I waited for Terrie to come for me but she didn't show up. I really wanted to see what was going on out there. I heard Millie and George's names announced several times. Marcie and Frosty placed quite often, too. That was when I learned my big brother's full name was RBF's Frosty Britches. It took me a few more shows to figure out that one of the adults always kept an eye on the children.

Sugar also won the two-year-old pleasure class. The win seemed to make her trainer and her owner both much happier, but not Sugar. She was so tired that she only wanted to sleep. I saw a whole different side of Marcie later that evening. She and Terrie were leading Frosty and me back from the wash rack when Sugar's trainer came over to introduce himself. I remember whispering to Sugar "Bumper Davis is a strange sounding name." He had come to talk with Terrie and look me over. He wanted to buy me!

Frosty whispered what the word "buy" meant. My blood nearly froze with dread and I was about to start my prayers to the horse guardians, but Marcie butted in to the negotiations. *"Terrie, don't even think about it! If you need money, or can't keep her, I'll buy her. I would rather see her go for dog food than end up with a horse beater like Bumper."*

I was sort of relieved when Marcie said she would buy me, because it meant I could stay at my new home. My relief was very short-lived, however. The idea crossed my horsey brain that maybe I had caused too much trouble during the year since I took up residence at the farm. I had really been afraid she wanted to make dog food out of me!

Sunday morning brought a different judge and different results. Sugar and I swapped places again. I was happy that my friend won if I couldn't, and being named champion put her humans in a much better mood. I was correct in my speculation of the previous day; Terrie was as pleased with my second place and reserve champion status. She seemed happy with me, and I hoped her joy would be enough to keep me from being sold to some nasty person or ending up as a doggie dinner.

I was really on my best behavior the rest of that summer. No kicking or biting irritating butts. No bucking when Terrie stepped on to my back, and believe me, keeping from exploding took a lot of willpower. When the Labor Day Appaloosa show rolled around, I was standing quietly as Terrie mounted and dismounted and had a pretty good handle on walk, trot, and whoa on command at home.

My efforts to back in sort of a straight line were improving, and I was guiding around pretty good. Terrie was almost as proud of me as I was of myself.

Sugar and I had not been stalled near each other since June when Marcie threatened to buy me to feed to the dogs. Truthfully, I missed chatting with my friend, but I was relieved that Sugar's owner and her trainer were not close to me. They appeared to have an adverse effect on Marcie. It occurred to me that Frosty's human was as aggressive, confrontational, and as unwilling to back down as I was. I thanked my lucky stars that Terrie had a more moderate personality. Labor Day weekend Sugar and I were side by side again.

That September outing was the first time Terrie rode me away from home. She walked me around the smaller warm up pen while I gawked at all the other horses with people on their backs. I'd been exposed to a similar sight on a much smaller scale at home, and lately I'd been working with Marcie and Frosty. George would ride Cutter and join us on occasion. I was pretty relaxed at home, but this small arena—though much larger than the one at home—was really crowded. I was getting cranky with the other horses buzzing by me. Many of them came really close to my backend before they passed me. I laid my ears back and swished my tail at them. "Back off!" I warned them.

Then most of the other horses and their riders left to go to the large arena where we'd shown at halter earlier that morning. Sugar and her rider entered the small arena with us. She'd won our halter class and was named champion; I was right behind her and stood reserve. That was how it went every time we showed together, one of us won and the other placed second. She told me earlier that she was in something called a two-year-old snaffle bit futurity.

"What's that?" I had asked her.

She wasn't sure. "I guess it's a special riding class. All the humans at my barn are talking about is *'futurity this, and futurity that.'* Like the halter futurities, they pay money to nominate the horses before the first of the calendar year. Payments are made to keep their entries in the futurities eligible to participate. The winner and top placers win the money that's been collected. Now you know as much as I do."

A lot of the tension eased from my body when Sugar joined the merry-go-round. Around and around we went, at a walk and a trot, and then someone would yell, *"Reverse."* At that point, we started the whole process over in the opposite direction. Thank the great horse gods! I was really getting dizzy.

We'd barely started in the new direction when Patch entered into the fray. My little brother was already carrying his human on his back!

He spotted me right away. "Hey, Love, isn't this wild?"

"Yeah, wild and a little scary, too!" I shouted back.

"You'll get used to it," Sugar added. Her attempt to ease our concerns got her spanked by her trainer. Both Patch's human and Terrie ignored our nervous outbursts.

Patch and I walked around, and we trotted a little, too. Sugar, however, was doing a very slow version of a gallop. I think Marcie had called it a *"lope."* Patch and I left the craziness when the place started to get crowded again. Sugar was still working. She was really tired when she finally made it back to her stall.

Sugar won her pleasure class and the futurity the following day. She referred to her trainer as "Bummer-D," and he was taking all the credit for her wins. He bragged to anyone who would listen, and he was always peeking at me from Sugar's stall. He gave me the creeps. On a brighter note, Patch won all his halter classes and the yearling stallion futurity. I did okay, placing right behind Sugar that weekend and went home with two reserve champion junior mare awards. Our horse family sure made an impact at that show.

Little did I know at the time, but that show was to forever change my budding show career. Terrie, Marcie, and George had struck up a friendship with Patch's owner, whose name turned out to be Jessie. In the course of their conversations, they discovered that Patch and I were full brother and sister. Right. So what?

It turned out that Patch was double registered. His name and pedigree was not only in the Appaloosa Stud Books, but also in the Rangerbred registry. I asked Frosty. "What's a Rangerbred?"

"I don't know, little sister. It must be a bloodline traced through your mother."

That made sense, I guess, because everyone decided since Patch was registered I should be too! I forgot about the whole issue once I got home, and everything in my life started coming unglued.

5
Advanced Training

My walk, trot, stop and back were humming right along. I stood quietly while Terrie mounted and dismounted. I was even negotiating a ground pole or two. The remainder of September went along and then became cool. I got a little silly as the leaves began to fall and blow around. Periodically, I was sure that a big monster lurked around one corner of the work arena. I would shy, shake my head, hop around a little, and run a few steps whenever it popped up.

Terrie quit riding me! She started to ride Frosty, and Marcie climbed into my saddle. On our first workout she said, "Okay, *Gunny, playtime is over.*" I wondered what terrible thing I'd done for Terrie to turn me over to Frosty's human.

My big brother warned me, "You hurt Marcie and you'll deal with me."

"That's not very helpful!" I grumbled as Marcie and I trotted past him and Terrie. I was a nervous wreck already and figured if I messed up with Marcie my next stop was the dog food option.

Our next few workouts were without any company, and I was getting fairly comfortable with Marcie's shorter legs and her more aggressive style of riding. Then, one of those big monsters showed up! I shied and tried to run away. Big mistake!

"*Okay, silly girl. You want to run? Let's run.*" She said and gave me a crack on the butt with her long reins. I objected to the spanking, which Terrie had never inflicted on me. I let out a little buck in protest. I got smacked again! That time I tried to run out from the sting on my hindquarters. Marcie didn't try to stop me. In fact, whenever I wanted to slow down, she applied the end of the reins again and made a smooching sound. I was exhausted and forgot all about the monster thing. It had been such a relief when she sat back in the saddle, took her legs off of my sides, and said whoa! I stopped so fast that my back hooves slid up under me, and my tail dragged in the sand.

Marcie patted my neck, and told me I was a good girl. She dismounted, loosened my girth, gave me another pat on my neck, and then led me into the barn.

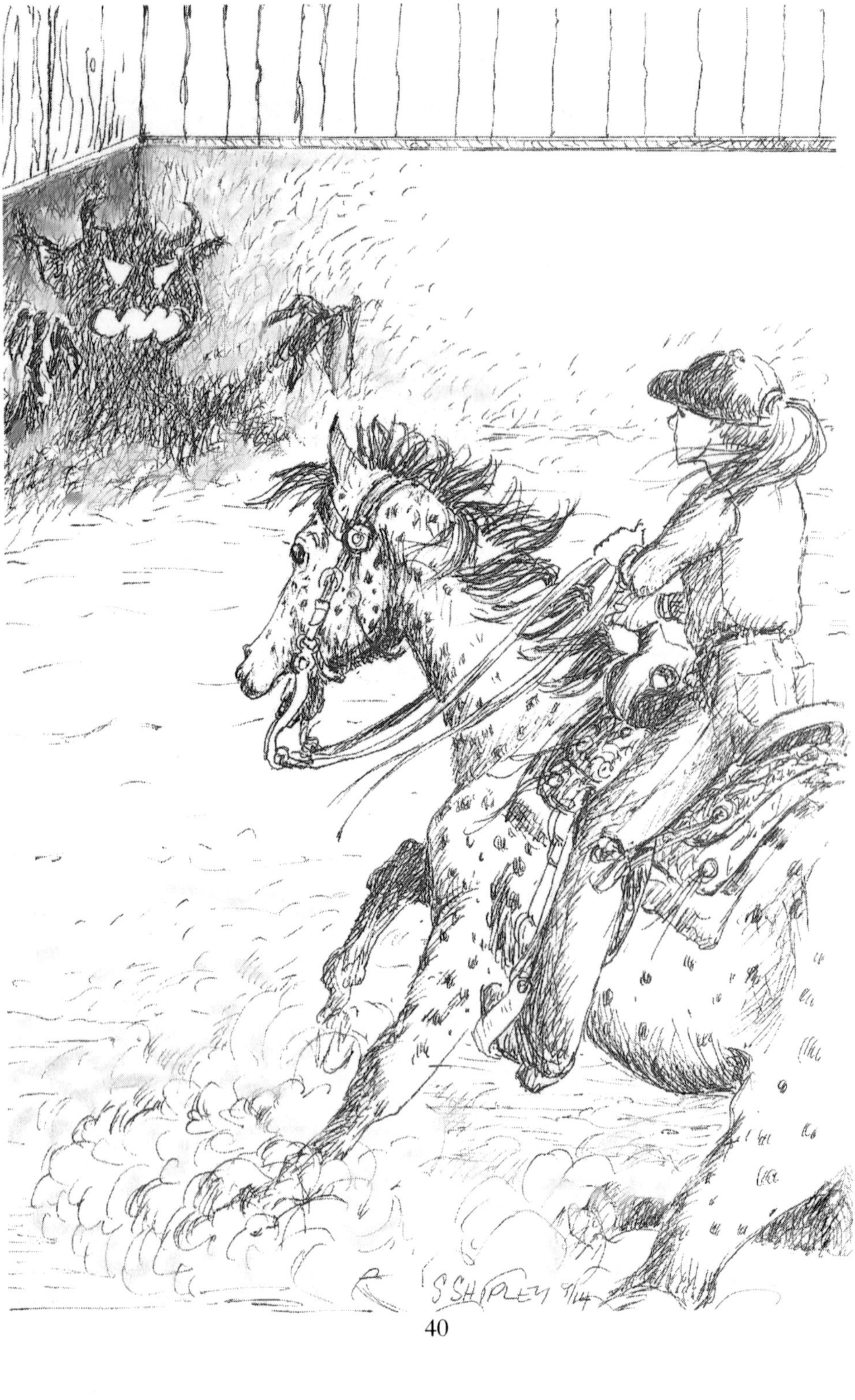
S SHIPLEY 9/14

She removed my working gear, toweled me off, put a long blanket-like thing on me that she called a cooler. Then she walked me around until I was breathing normal. Marcie groomed and blanketed me before I was returned to my stall.

After our first ride, Marcie started carrying what Frosty told me was a dressage whip. The whip could tickle my sides, but it did smart more than the crack of the reins when she spanked my rear end. I quickly learned how to canter with only a squeeze of her legs, which eliminated any need for the whip reinforcement.

We had been turned out in a light snowfall. It took me a while to work up enough nerve to ask Frosty why Terrie had stopped riding me and traded with Marcie. "What did I do to make her not want me?"

"Terrie still wants you. She has a little trouble trusting a young horse at a canter. She had a bad fall with a three-year-old gelding she'd been training before she brought you home, and I guess it still effects her."

"Do you think she'll come back to me when I learn more?" I hoped that Terrie would still want me. Frosty and Marcie had a special bond, and I wondered if I would ever have such a relationship with a human.

Things were progressing well as the trees lost the last of their leaves, or so I thought. Terrie took over my lunge-line work, and she rode me a couple of times a week in addition to the schooling that Marcie continued. I got a day off only when it rained or an early snow storm blew in.

Frosty tried to warn me. "Don't be surprised or worried when you're taken away for the winter."

"What do you mean by taken away?" His comment didn't make sense to me.

"The footing is getting bad in our workout arena, and I overheard Terrie and Marcie discussing moving you to a boarding stable for the winter, so they could continue your education."

Sure enough, the following week I was moved to a larger barn with an indoor riding arena attached. It was like being at a horse show with many strange horses and people; the lighted arena was flanked by box stalls on either side. A week went by without any show classes. At that point, I realized I was not going home.

Terrie or George arrived each morning to turn me outside whenever the sun overcame the rain or snow. They lunged me or chased me around in the covered arena when it was too nasty for me to go outdoors. Marcie also made an appearance each evening to ride me.

I learned to transition through my gaits more smoothly, back up straighter, and stand quietly to wait for her next command. Marcie didn't humor me much when the devil sat on my shoulder; she was all business and more stubborn than I was, so we butted heads on occasion.

Though my official birthday is in April, the first of the year all horses advance by one year if they show or race. New Years Day I moved on to three-year-old status, and Terrie disappeared from my daily workout routine. Marcie said, *"Terrie got married and went on a honeymoon."* I didn't know what that meant, but I missed her.

Marcie and I had the arena to ourselves most of the time that winter. The other working horse and rider teams never amounted to more than three or four. As a result, I was unprepared for the chaos of an early spring schooling show. The schooling show madness was much worse than the make-up ring free-for-all at the Appaloosa show the previous fall. Either the people riding the other horses were crazy, or the horses were.

I pinned my ears back, flagged my tail, and warned the invaders of my personal space "Back off or get thumped!" I told them. One pint-size gelding didn't heed my warning and ran smack into my rear end. I kicked him in the chest, and Marcie spanked me with the reins and poked me in the sides with her spurs! I snorted and shook my head in protest, but I knew better than to buck.

"Bad girl!" Marcie scolded. *"You could have hurt the child riding that pony. We need to get a handle on this situation."*

So, for the rest of that show and a half dozen more schooling shows, Marcie rode me two handed and carried the darn dressage whip. Every time I put my ears back and cranked my tail, I got smacked. A pot shot at one of the other horses had caused me to be spanked harder in addition to being stuck with her spurs. It would be another decade before I appreciated Marcie's strict discipline and understood that she wasn't abusing me. She had only used the spurs or whip when I got hardheaded or disobedient.

Marcie and George were pretty pleased with my saddle training. Their only complaint had been my aggressive behavior in the riding classes. I was relieved when Frosty and Millie joined me for the Memorial Day Appaloosa show.

That three-day show had turned out to be like old home week. Sugar and Patch showed up, as well as Blue. She'd grown a lot since the last time I had seen her. At our first reunion since our childhood, a gray haired gentleman showed Blue at halter, and then he coached his granddaughter in showmanship.

Terrie popped up on day two in the company of a dark haired man with a bearded face and nervous brown eyes. It was obvious he was not comfortable around us horses. "City dude," Frosty snorted. And I wondered what that meant.

Terrie posted a sign on my stall before she left, and Marcie tore it down as soon as she was gone. Then she sent George and Kelly to check out the bulletin boards and the information table in the entry office for more sale flyers.

Marcie was saddling me up for a warm up before our pleasure class the following day when an elderly couple stopped by to look at me. I listened to Marcie explain to the disappointed folks that she had purchased me the night before.

The other horses had warned me that I made too much trouble for Terrie and sooner or later she would get rid of me. I was on my best behavior in my pleasure class and went home with a blue ribbon. I hadn't placed on the first day, but managed to snag a sixth on day two. Day three of the show I moved up to second place. Marcie gave me a pat and an apple at the end of each day.

Marcie wasn't in the habit of giving me treats. "Frosty, why did she give me an apple? Is she fattening me up for the dog food buyers?"

He snorted and laughed. "No, silly, you belong to Marcie and George now, like the rest of us. We always get an apple after a long day of showing." I filed his response away with other important things to remember. Terrie used to give me carrots and always left a bag for me, but it was George who made sure I got one when Terrie wasn't there.

As the Independence Day show rolled around I had several more wins in my western pleasure class, and Marcie entered me in something called a command class. It took me a while to figure it out. The trick was to do immediately whatever the announcer said. Frosty had given me a few pointers. "Don't ever listen to the click of the microphone. Just pay attention to what Marcie tells you. On the command to stop, don't move a muscle."

Twenty-two of us entered that class, by Marcie's count, and nearly half of the horses were eliminated before we reversed direction. Once the disqualified group left, the class resumed. We lost three more on the command to extend our trot and two fell out of contention on the counter canter. I messed up on the side pass away from the rail, picking up my canter lead instead. We ended up with sixth place. Everyone was acting like I'd won the class, so I guess I did okay.

In between show outings, I learned the side-pass from the rail and to backup straight until I was told halt. There was a very subtle difference between the leg cues for the side-pass and those for the canter. Marcie helped me understand by adding a smooching sound for the canter. I also learned to plant my inside leg and spin around in both directions.

Late fall Marcie finally relented and let little Kara begin to practice showmanship with me. We practiced, practiced, and practiced some more under Marcie and George's supervision.

Kara's wise parents picked small local schooling shows for our first few of outings. Marcie went over the showmanship patterns to make sure five-year-old Kara understood what was required. Okay, so she led me from the wrong side after the judge did his walk around and sent us back to the lineup, but overall we did great! And that is exactly what our coach, Kara's mom, told her. Three schooling shows later we placed third out of ten. I'd found my special human. Marcie and George were announced as my owners at the shows in those days. But little Kara owned my heart, and I could tell she loved me too.

Kara and I were doing very well as a team in showmanship classes, so George and Marcie decided that we were going to something called the C.R.H.A National Show the following September.

The year I turned four, Marcie added reining to my growing list of performance classes at Appaloosa shows. Kara and I continued to improve our showmanship technique. We also paired up to compete in the lead line class and were becoming serious competitors.

Shortly following our first Colorado Ranger Horse Association (C.R.H.A.) National Show I was off to a new winter boarding facility. My C.R.H.A. adventures and the curse associated with those outings require special attention, but I will share those memories with you later in my tale.

The boarding stable, in neighboring Hinckley, would become my second home for the following two years. Frosty accompanied me to the indoor workout sessions the winter I turned seven. That was a winter I have never forgotten.

6
Skunks Galore!

As had become my habit whenever disembarking from the horse trailer, I announced my arrival. "Hey, everyone I'm back!" I'd Shout. Marcie never hollered at me for shouting near her ear, like Terrie had. Marcie only shook her head. She ignored my exuberant greetings because she figured it was part of what she called my "quirky personality." Well...the fact that Kara and I were really hitting it off might have had a lot to do with her patience in regard to my vocal outbursts.

George unloaded Frosty and followed us into the aisle-way between the two box stall rows, to remove our shipping boots. Okay! Hold on here. George put Frosty into the stall I'd been occupying since my first winter at Achin' Acres Farm. I snorted in protest as Marcie walked me down the smaller aisle that connected the main barn with the indoor arena. I stopped to gape at the changes that had occurred since I'd left there early last spring. Two newer looking box stalls had been erected at the far end of the arena from where the door to the human's lounge was located. I was put in the second stall. The first stall was tucked into the corner, and an old gelding called it home. I think he was black, but—like me—he was wearing a winter blanket and hood. The hay and bedding was stored on the opposite side of my new stall. That whole end of the arena was blocked off from the rest of the workspace with some kind of temporary fence.

I had been sort of bummed out when Marcie left me there, so I was not interested in chitchat. My new neighbor moved close to the wall that separated us and tried to initiate a conversation. "Hi there! My name is Stormy. What do your humans call you?"

"My human family call me Gunny, and if you want to find out how I got that nickname, just keep annoying me."

"Sorry. I came in here last week, and it's been lonely without another horse to talk with."

I felt bad for unloading my nasty mood on him, so I relented. "We can talk later. At the moment I'm upset that my brother got the nice warm stall in the upper barn, and I'm stuck down here."

"It's not so bad. I've been entertaining myself by watching people work with some of the other horses and ponies."

Stormy was absolutely correct we had a ringside view of all the horse shenanigans. It had been much the same watching the kids in the warm-up ring at the 4-H shows. Kara and I had a lot of help from Marcie when we hit rough patches, but some of the kids evidently didn't have very much help.

I knew instruction was available at my winter home because Marcie had worked me with the aid of the stable boss in past winters. I discussed some of my observations with my brother when we were turned out in the arena a few days after our arrival. I also had to lodge a protest with him about Kara. She had been pulled from riding me and given to Frosty. I snorted at him and flattened my ears.

"What straw do you have stuck up your butt, now?" he asked.

"You already have your own human. Why do you have to steal my Kara?"

"I've been carting Kara around and helping Marcie teach her how to ride since she turned three. That was before you showed up at our farm and long before you were even saddle broke."

I thought his answer over and then came up with a plan. The trick was how to convince Frosty. "Kara and I are a team, and we have a special connection like you and Marcie. I would gladly trade you Marcie back for Kara!"

He laughed at me! But when he saw how disappointed I was that he didn't like my plan, he explained, "I'm only helping Kara's mother teach her how to canter and start over fences. Marcie will be training you, so that you are ready when Kara comes back to you."

That information placated me some, and I wasn't quite as bummed out. Marcie worked me in the mornings, and coached Kara on Frosty after school hours. I took it all in. What could he do that I couldn't? After all, my little human had been riding me hunt seat the whole previous season at all kinds of shows, and we did really well. A little disclaimer is due here: Marcie did usually work my butt off before Kara was allowed on my back.

Kara was doing a good job of picking up a canter and transitioning back to the trot. We'd been there slightly over a month when Marcie started adding ground poles to our workouts. At first we merely walked through two, and then three poles. No sweat! I handled them fine, but Marcie widened the distance between the poles and we had to trot through them. She added two more poles, to what she referred to as cavaletti, as the winter wore on and fewer riders filled the arena.

Frosty made it look easy to trot through the ground poles. He planted each hoof smack between each of the poles. Well...I thought it wouldn't be a problem to negotiate two more poles. WRONG! I stepped on the third one with my front hoof and stumbled through the last two. At that moment, I'd been grateful that Marcie had chosen to work me in the morning when no one else was around. Stormy was the only one who witnessed my bumbling attempt to trot through the five poles. Marcie asked me to try again after she reset the poles. That attempt was a complete disaster. I stumbled over the poles and sent them flying like giant pick up sticks!

Marcie took me back to three poles for a long time. As our gymnastics continued to progress, she raised the poles off of the ground a few inches for Frosty, but mine remained safely on flat ground.

I told him one day, "I'm really getting depressed watching you and Kara work over the cavaletti. She's never going to want to come back to me. I stumbled so badly that I almost fell down, and Marcie has me back to three ground poles while you cruise through five raised ones."

"Relax. You're trying too hard," he said.

His reaction seemed strange, Stormy had told me the very same thing after the five-pole debacle. They were probably right, I was in a hurry to learn and get my Kara back.

A few nights following my conversation with Frosty I had been munching the last of my hay. The hour was late and all the lights were out when Stormy whispered to me. "Psst! Hey, Gunny, don't' make any quick moves. There's a pole cat in the arena."

"What's a pole cat?" I asked.

"A skunk!"

I scanned the arena floor until I picked up the shadowy form of a small black critter with the white stripe on its back and tail. It made its way toward the small opening the cats used to enter and leave the lounge with the big viewing window that overlooked the work area. "What's it doing, Stormy?"

"Probably, stealing the cat's food. I sure hope no one goes in the room while it's there. They can sure raise a terrible stink when they're upset, and the odor hangs around for a long time."

We watched that skunk make its nightly trip for nearly two weeks. Then Skunky disappeared for a while. She reappeared not only to steal the cat's food, but several of its newborns. One kitten at a time was carted across the arena and disappeared near the tack room located just out of our sight in the short aisle way to the main barn.

The humans were hunting for the missing kittens the following day. Only Stormy and I knew the fate of the feline babies.

We all went back to work and forgot about the little skunk thief. Kara was now trotting Frosty over three poles and a pop over cross bar jump. I was up to three raised poles. Marcie seemed reluctant to give me five again, even when the poles were on the ground, but she let me try the cross bar. I kind of walked through it on my first try, so she raised the height of the jump a little. The next try I jumped it like it was a huge Olympic style fence, and I scared the poop out of both of us. However, I did manage to entertain Stormy enough to get a good horselaugh out of him.

The weather warmed up enough for us to have our workouts outside for nearly a week before the snow staged a comeback. It was a nice break from the arena and the darn ground poles. Kara and I had begun to hone our showmanship skills on weekends. She was also working with Frosty, but instead of using a halter she was practicing with him wearing his English bridle. What the heck was that about? I wondered. They were trotting a lot faster than was usual for showmanship practice.

The moment I think I have a good handle on things, something else pops up to confuse me. Frosty had been working with Kara and Marcie on what I found out was hunt seat style showmanship, and now it was my turn. Everything was pretty much the same as what Kara and I had been doing at the Appaloosa shows; I only had to trot a lot faster.

Kara and I got a chance to practice our new form of showmanship a few weeks later. We participated in a clinic held at our winter digs. Well…I guess we may need a little more work; I trotted a bit fast and missed Kara's cue to turn at one of the designated places in the pattern. She left me after the showmanship mess up and went back to Frosty for the hunt seat classes. I sat there alone in my stall and watched my little person ride my brother. Stormy was also out in the arena practicing with his human, and I didn't have anyone to listen to my complaints.

All the kids at the barn showed up earlier each day the following week. Kelly had been working with Millie at home whenever the weather permitted. During spring break, he rode me after Marcie finished my regular workout. Kelly refused to ride in the hunt saddle, so I was transformed back into a western mount while Kara and Frosty continued to work on their hunter routine.

Adults seem to moderate their language whenever children are around, and perhaps that added to my confusion when I heard polecats mentioned. Marcie and the stable owner were having a strange conversation while we carted the kids around the arena.

"Marcie, take whatever you can home with you," the barn boss told her.

"What's up, Ellen?"

Ellen looked at the young riders circling them and cleared her throat before answering. *"There've been a string of thefts at local boarding stables and show barns. The polecats are only taking the best saddles, bridles, and show halters."*

"Okay. Thanks for the heads up. We'll cart our tack back and forth from home for a while."

The human language can be a challenge to a horse. We are much more adept at reading their body language and voice inflection. To me, the word polecat was another description of a skunk, and I couldn't figure out how that little cat size critter could manage to cart off our tack. It appeared to have had enough trouble handling the tiny kittens. We were walking side by side during our cool down, so I asked Frosty. "How the heck can a polecat steal a saddle?"

"I'm sure the little skunks can't, but I think polecat was a metaphor for human thieves."

I thought about his answer and decided it made more sense than the little black striped critter attempting to handle a saddle.

The barn quieted down after the little humans returned to school. My blanket was getting itchy as my coat shed beneath it. I was busy scratching my butt on the stall wall when I caught several small shadows crossing the arena floor, in the predawn darkness. The small parade was led by the little skunk thief. Two considerably larger kittens that were almost the size of their foster mom closely followed her through the small cat entrance to the lounge. A short time later, the trio emerged from the lounge and retraced their steps. Stormy and I kept our eyes on them until they disappeared into the tack room.

"Hey Stormy. What do you think they were up to in there?"

"Skunky is probably teaching her peculiar family where to find food. She is most likely getting ready to wean them."

The next couple of nights the two kittens and their skunk mamma repeated the raid on the cat's food bowl. On the forth night, another kitten joined the parade. It was mostly white and much smaller than its darker colored siblings. However, it appeared to grow stronger over the next week and was better able to keep up with the others.

Stormy and I had gotten used to the routine of the strange family, and we were dozing off when we heard a ruckus in the main barn. Frosty let out a bellow that shook the rafters. "Strangers in the barn!" It wasn't like my big brother to be upset about humans he didn't know entering the boarding stable. I was about to ask him what he was all upset about when I saw strange light beams bouncing along the aisleway from the main barn to the tack room around the corner from where Stormy and I were stalled. We watched the blue white beams come closer. I knew the beams were from flashlights. George and Marcie used them whenever a storm knocked out the power, but there hadn't been any storms lately. Frosty bellowed again, "Polecats! Polecats in the barn." Then he blasted the side of his stall with his powerful hind hooves.

About the same time, he made that declaration the little ones and their foster mom appeared from their late night meal and started for their usual exit. Frosty was soon joined in his uproar by some angry stable mates he'd woken from their slumber. The human thieves quickened their pace and grabbed a couple of more saddles before making a hasty exit. It's, hard to say whether the human polecats didn't see the small kittens, in the darkness, or one of the nasty fellows deliberately kicked one of them. Whatever, the kitten let out a yowl that was quickly followed by human wails and curses. Mamma took exception to the treatment of her adopted kittens and sprayed the humans attempting to make off with the saddles.

I snorted and tried to clear the smell from my nostrils. "Wow! You sure weren't kidding, Stormy, when you said skunks could raise a real stink."

"Yeah, and those human skunks won't be able to hide anywhere for long."

Stormy sure had that right. The stable owner called the police when she woke to the uproar started by Frosty, and she had noticed a strange vehicle parked in front of the barn. The responding officers nabbed the driver on his way out the drive with a load of stolen tack. The two human skunks still in the barn tried to escape out the back door, but a canine officer had no trouble tracking them down.

Little Skunky and Frosty were the unsung heroes of the capture of the saddle thieves. One evening, the skunk snuck out while her cat kittens were busy eating. Everyone was happy to see the kittens; however, they did stink a bit. I was sure the smell would fade from the kittens quicker than it could wear off the tack room and some of the tack that had inadvertently been sprayed on the night of the botched saddle heist. From that day on
I always walked softly and held my breath whenever I crossed paths with those little black and white cat like critters. Human skunks are another problem that can crop up at unexpected times in a horse's life.

7
Who's a Pony?

Kara and I became a full time team the year she turned twelve. I was ten that spring and fairly accomplished, which turned out to be a fortunate turn of events. We were competing in canter classes after almost two years of being limited to walk trot classes at Appaloosa and open shows. Kara rode me most of the time, and I had to tolerate Marcie only on occasion.

Trail riding had become an enhanced enjoyment for me with Kara in the saddle. She didn't grumble when I stepped out of the trailer and then asked, "Hello, is there anyone out there that I know?" Sometimes a friend would answer me, or a new horse would introduce itself. It seemed I got a lot more response at the horse shows.

That spring Marcie signed up Kara and me for lessons at local hunter jumper barn. We started on the usual cavaletti and crossbars, but within a few lessons, we advanced to navigating actual jump courses. The fences were different, because of things called coops that looked like a small peaked roof that had been placed on the ground between winged uprights. The uprights were still referred to as standards, and they held rubber cups to support the jump poles. However, unlike the pole standards I was used to, the wing standards were at least two feet wide, and they had the appearance of small gates. The brush jump looked like an evergreen yard hedge, and the roll top resembled giant barrels that had been cut in half and the top carpeted in green. Both of those jumps were topped with a regular jump pole, which made it easier to judge their height on approach. The jumps also included a pole set on the ground on either side. The humans used the term ground poles and ground lines interchangeably. Whatever the name, the poles on the ground occupied a space about half the height of the jump.

I have to admit that at first they were very intimidating. Thankfully, Marcie insisted the instructor keep us at a reasonable height of three feet, but some of those obstacles were three to four feet wide. Okay, Kara and I mastered those scary jumps, and by mid-summer, we were sailing over them. We were always on the correct lead when landing and approaching the next fence, thanks to all the work we had done at home. We continued to take lessons once a weak throughout that summer and practiced our varied routines at home.

We cleaned up in the novice over fences and hunt seat equitation over fences at the 4-H shows.

Marcie signed us up for Pony Club following fair that year. Once a week, I hopped into the trailer and went on a new kind of trail ride. Later, I learned our new outdoor challenge was referred to as a cross-country hunter course, which had natural looking obstacles for us to conquer. The jumps spanned long spaces and included several height variations. Ponies and less experienced horses could opt for the lower heights while the more experienced hunters sailed over jumps in excess of four feet.

There was usually a meeting and a short warm up before each outing. At the end of the second week workout, our leader commented on Kara's nice pony. I was looking around and trying to find this pony that was replacing me when Kara informed the Pony Club leader, *"Gunny is an Appaloosa horse!"* She had sounded upset. I was kind of relieved there was not a new pony, but, all the same, like Kara, I was insulted. Ponies lived at the boarding stable where I spent my winters, and they were very prevalent at 4-H shows. The ponies I had experience with were small equines. As it turned out, the folks at the Pony Club called any ladies or children's mount a pony. It confused me that the small ponies as well as the huge warmbloods were referred to as ponies. I don't think Kara could figure that one out either. We both calmed down. After that, we stopped taking the nice pony comments as some kind of personal prejudice aimed at my spotted hide.

The following winter should have been a warning of the year to come. Kara and I worked at home until close to Christmas before moving to our winter home at the boarding stable. It was the first winter I could remember working outdoors while in residence there. The early spring of 1988 was hot and dry, but I was cranking on all cylinders, super fit and raring to go.

 We had continued throughout the winter to go to Pony Club workouts, which allowed us to make use of the large indoor arena.

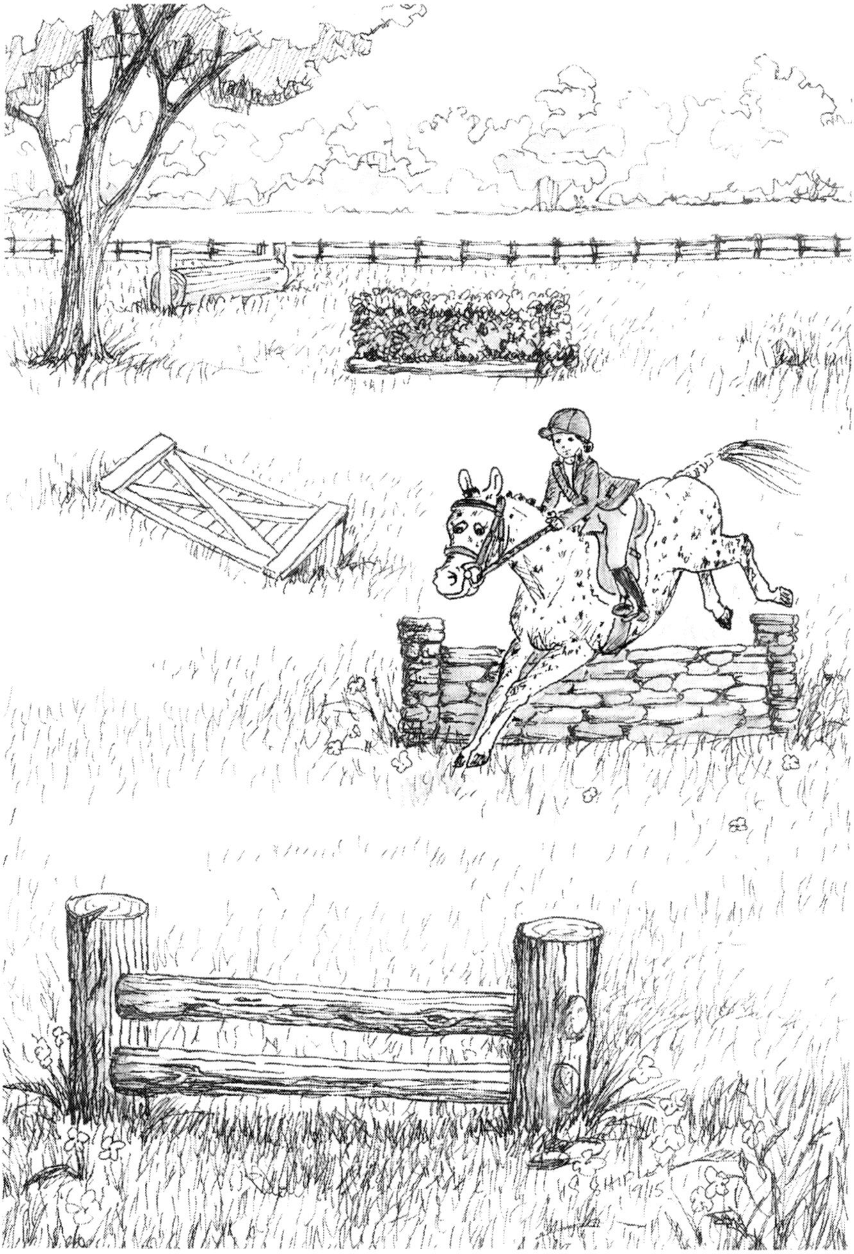

The leader of the group erected a jump course for us to practice. The owners held several clinics at the farm where we attended our club workouts. Two of the guest instructors coached us over fences, but the third clinician introduced us to something called dressage. You guessed it. Kara loved it, and in early May dressage was added to our 4-H project list.

I started out as a western horse and had amassed wins in halter, showmanship, western pleasure, and trail class. But my education and skill sets didn't stop there: Marcie taught me to rein. She helped Kara and me learn how to master western riding. She coached Kara on the more simplified 4-H reining patterns, and my little partner did a heck of a job remembering the patterns. Her ability to memorize a course was a good thing too. Not only did the hunter classes require her to remember a new pattern for each class we entered, but the dressage inclusion also required designated maneuvers. The tests were similar to the reining patterns and the required moves had to be completed as written. Patterns were listed for the reining and dressage 4-H events in the rulebook or project books. The Pony Club had their own handbook with several levels of dressage tests.

Kara had her heart set on something called a versatility class that was held at the 4-H championship show during our county fair, and I had no idea what that meant or what was involved, but I was soon to find out.

4-Hers entered classes one at a time during the wicked heat, and youngsters became ill from the unusually high temperatures that summer. We were in the middle of a drought, and many of my horse friends also suffered from the heat. Some had bouts of colic from excessive work and not enough water. I had been showing Monday thru Thursday nonstop, at the junior fair horse show. I was in top condition, but after every class Marcie made Kara and me go into a shady spot to await our next class. Frosty's human made sure that her daughter and I were cooled down and drank plenty of water. Thursday was the championship show where the top placing rider and horse teams competed for Champion in each age group and division. Those same riders qualified to enter the Versatility Class, which included Kara and yours truly.

As I recall, we entered the English Pleasure part of the versatility madness under bright lights that lit up the night. I knew there was a large crowd in the bleachers, on the grassy hill, and seated at picnic tables that encircled the show ring. I sensed the gathered spectators more than saw them; we were in the spotlight and they were on the dark periphery. We worked both ways of the ring, and then lined up in the center of the arena where we usually received our placing and whatever ribbons we had earned. The entrance and exit gates opened. Crazy people pushed wheelbarrows loaded with saddles and clothes. On the run, these folks picked out their horse and rider then came to a halt in front of them.

Marcie took my reins while George stripped my saddle, and Kara was busy changing her boots and cinching on her chaps. My western saddle and bridle in place and Kara remounted on my back we went back out to the rail to wait for the rest of the class to make their changes. Western pleasure went much the same as the previous class, and I was expecting another charge of the wheelbarrow brigade. Marcie and George came in to place my splint boots on my front legs and skid boots on my back ones. Marcie toweled me off while George sprayed more fly repellant to my sweaty coat. At that point, they exited the show pen.

Our pleasure class was over, and we all went to the end of the arena, near the gates. We were called one at a time to perform a reining pattern. Kara and I had a few reining classes to our credit, so we were relatively relaxed while we waited our turn to run. The strange thing was that we never left the arena, and we had been in there over an hour by the time half of the class had completed their patterns.

Once more, the brigade of grooms invaded. Several horses had their bridles changed again. The last part of that versatility trial was a series of three barrels. I watched closely as the ring crew set them up in a triangle. One was placed to the right of where we stood, one to the left, and the third was placed at the far end in the center of the arena. We watched the first four horses run toward the right barrel turn around it on the right lead. Then each of them ran to the other side and turned to the left. Every one of them ran to the barrel planted in the middle of the arena, turned to the left, and then hightailed to the finish line. A particularly speedy gelding kept on coming, and I thought he was going to crash into the rest of us. The cloverleaf barrels appeared to be a timed event; the faster the time better a horse and rider placed. I found out the event was barrel racing, but if you turned the wrong way on your run or knocked down a barrel, you were eliminated.

Then our turn came. Kara put me into a canter and we loped to the first turn, loped to the second turn, and moseyed on down to the last turn. The crowd was shouting encouragement to Kara, "Run, Kara, run for home!" I circled the last barrel at a leisurely lope, and then my little rider asked me to run. I took off at a brisk canter. Most of the other horses ran the course somewhere between eighteen to twenty-five seconds. Our time was a whapping thirty-two seconds, but we went clean while many of the really fast horses knocked over a barrel or ran off. Our slow time may have moved us down in overall points, but we managed to snag a third out of eighteen. It's worth noting that Kara was the youngest rider competing in versatility that year.

It turned out to be a banner year for Kara and me as a horse and rider team. We were darned near perfect. We went to a few weekend shows that August, following our county fair.

George took the trailer to have it checked out following the Labor Day weekend show. I think he was trying to head off the annual curse, but a truck sideswiped our silver trailer before he got it home, which put an end to our showing for the year. Kara was heartbroken that we couldn't make the CRHA National Show that year, but I was relieved.

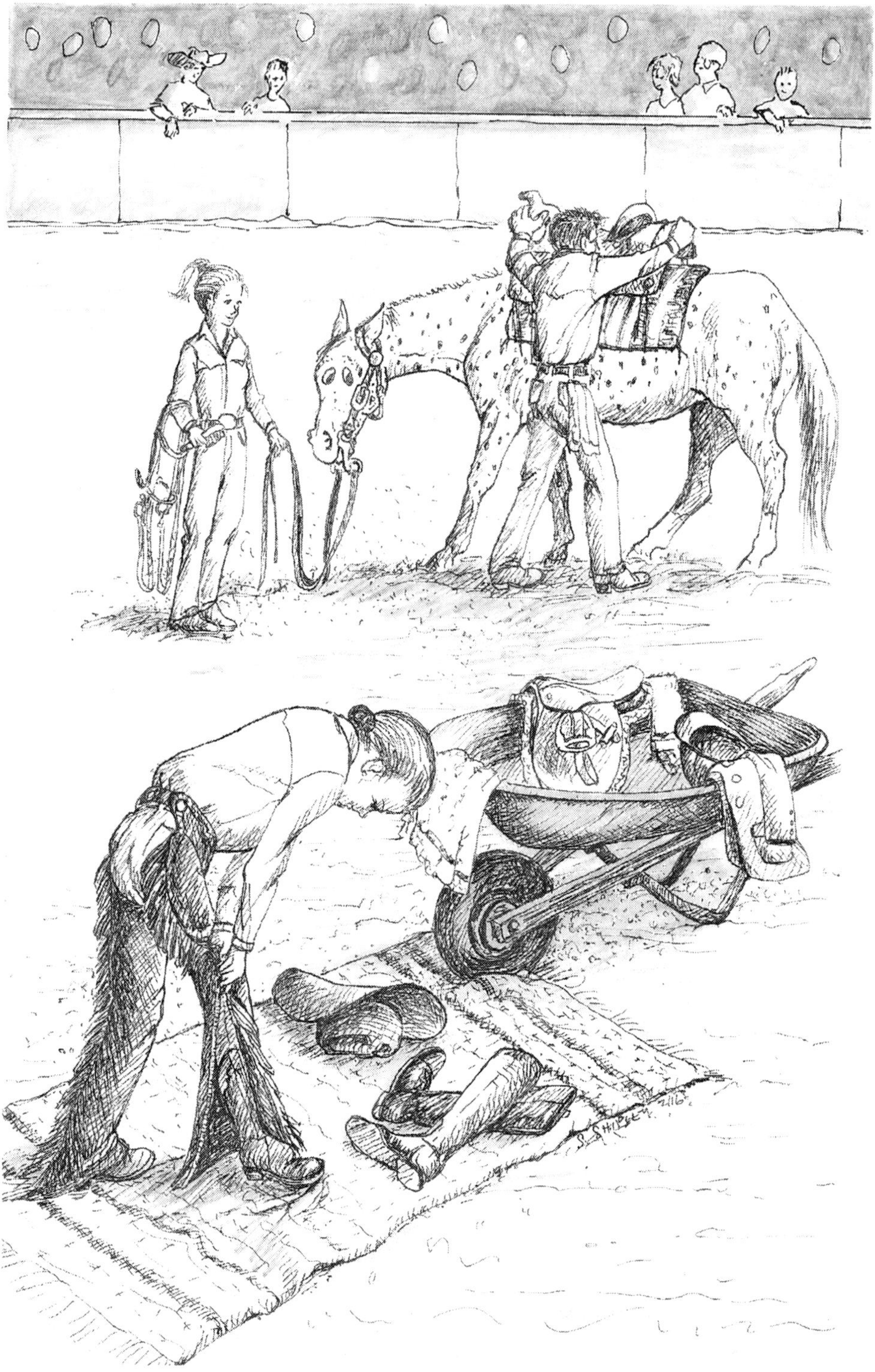

Typical Appaloosa Coat Patterns

Blanket-Any color with white over hips with spots

Blanket-Any color with white over hips no spots

Leopard-White with any color spots

Any color with white snowflake spots

Blue or Red Roan with Varnish Marks

Any color with white spots over hips

8
C.R.H.A. Adventures

The time is at hand for me to step back in the story of my life to share the bizarre circumstances surrounding my travels to the Colorado Ranger Horse Association National Shows.

My first misadventure occurred early September of my four-year-old year. My brother and Millie usually traveled with me, but not on that trip. I should have guessed something was up when I was loaded into Frosty's usual spot up front in the four horse trailer and the stall door was latched behind me. Thus began my first experience traveling to the C.R.H.A. National Show.

West Virginia:

A lot of firsts happened on that trip. I was lonely on that long haul to West Virginia. We were part of a caravan from Ohio, and all these decades later, I can't figure out who made the decision to travel the backroads or why. My trailer went up and down, it went left then sharp right, then plunged down and up again!

I sat on my rear end, thinking the position would help me balance. Honestly, I don't remember if it helped, but I don't think it did. However, sitting on the butt bar and the stall door made my tail sore and bald near the top. My disposition had turned sour by the time we arrived at our destination.

I was extremely unhappy with the whole experience and didn't call out my usual greeting. Instead, when my hooves were firmly planted on solid ground, my only interest was to put a huge distance between the trailer and my sore body. If I hadn't been indulging in my own pity party, I may have noticed a pair of malevolent eyes tracking our progress.

Marcie removed my leg wraps before she put me in a freshly bedded stall. My tail wrap had been rubbed off and trashed hours earlier. George filled my water bucket while I worked on my hay and Marcie put salve on my raw tail. *"That sure was a bad ride for you, girl. We will try a different route on the way home."*

I hadn't been in the mood to be placated. All I heard was, "Blah, blah, blah." For a response, I scrunched up my nose, flattened my ears on my neck, and showed her my crabby face.

Once my humans left the stall area, I took a snooze. Thirst roused me from my nap. I moseyed over to my water bucket, and stuck my muzzle into the water. One sip of the foul tasting liquid convinced me that someone was trying to poison me!

As you may recall, my brother Patch was registered as a Colorado Ranger Horse in addition to his Appaloosa status. As for me, I had mixed feelings about my new papers touting my pedigree listed in the volumes of the Colorado Ranger Horse Association stud books.

After my workout early the next morning, it was bath time. When Marcie and I arrived, Patch was already on the wash rack. He greeted me, "Howdy, Love. When did you get here?" I ignored him. "What straw do you have up your butt?" he asked me.

Well, I took my bad mood out on him. "YOU!"

"What did I do?" he inquired.

I shared my viewpoint with him. "My whole nightmare trip to this place with bad water is your fault."

He was genuinely puzzled. "How can it be my fault?"

I set him straight. "You and your double registered bragging. My humans wouldn't even know about this show if your human hadn't blabbed about us being full brother and sister." I showed him my ugliest expression.

He snorted. "You're mad at me for something my human did?"

"Don't try to rationalize with me!" I shouted back at him.

"Mares, they're all goofy." He said with a good deal of disgust.

His human walked him away while Marcie continued to bathe me.

My coat was squeaky clean. What was remained of my tail, and my undamaged mane flowed like strands of silk. Later that morning, Marcie and I waited to enter the show ring for my halter class. My disposition was nearly as crappy as it had been since our arrival. Marcie frowned at me, but I didn't care and continued to scrunch up my nose, pin my ears to the rear, and make the make the most terrible expressions possible.

Okay, so I blew my class at our first C.R.H.A. National Show. I was awarded fourth place for my mutiny. I guess the judge didn't like my sour disposition, which had been reflected by my crabby faces.

Halter classes concluded, and the showmanship classes were up next. I heard Marcie tell Kara to do her best and not worry about the place. Then she added, *"Gunny is in a bad mood and not her usual self."* Kara was my person, and I didn't want my stinky attitude to affect her, so, I perked my ears forward and made an extreme effort to look pleasant during our showmanship. My tiny handler got third; she was the youngest exhibitor in the ten and under class of twenty entries.

I put my ugly face back on along with my bad behavior for my riding classes later that Saturday afternoon. I hadn't had a drink in nearly two days and was severely dehydrated by Sunday morning, which made my experience more unbearable. Marcie cancelled our classes for the day. She and George took me home as soon as they packed up all the junk that goes with us to every outing.

Happy doesn't sound like the right word to describe how I felt when we arrived home, but being a horse my vocabulary is relatively limited.

My refusal to drink at the West Virginia show had prompted George and Marcie to haul huge containers of water from our home. The CRHA curse was in its early stages, and none of us had a clue of how bad it was going to get.

Ohio:

The following year should have gone easier. The National Show was in our home state of Ohio and only a short ride down the highway. The route was very familiar, to me, as were the show grounds. It had been the site of my first Appaloosa show where I found Sugar again and became better acquainted with my little brother. I was still bummed out at Patch, or more aptly, at his human for getting me into that debacle in West Virginia.

"Oh! Great horse god, please save a place for me," I prayed as a loud clank startled me. The initial noise was replaced with a scraping sound, and a horrifying roar marked our progress down the Interstate. That's how I arrived at my second C.R.H.A. National. The deafening fanfare woke every dozing soul and spooked many of the assembled Rangerbreds. I thought a low profile suited our entrance to the show grounds, so I didn't call out my usual greeting. My ears were still ringing, and I doubt that I could have heard any response.

I had been happy to be in one piece and safely in a clean stall with plenty of hay to munch. A dropped muffler system caused the terrible scraping noise and the resulting roar of our tow vehicle. George spent the first day of our CRHA outing administering first aid to our truck.

Marcie rode me on Friday night and early Saturday morning before the halter classes. I was more than willing to vacate my stall early. Horses arrived late into the night and the wee hours before day one of the show. My rest had been interrupted by what I thought was a nightmare. The guy Sugar referred to as Bummer D was casting his hateful gaze on me while I slept. Insomnia plagued me the remainder of the night, so I watched the horses and their humans as they located the stalls assigned to them.

I had not been very social at last years CRHA show in West Virginia. As a result, I didn't recognize the majority of the other Rangerbreds entering the barn. Finally Patch showed up, and Blue arrived shortly after.

We made it back home without further mishap. I remember being very thankful and extremely relieved to stretch out in my stall and catch up on some much needed sleep. I woke several times and scanned the dark recesses of the barn. I couldn't seem to shake the evil eyes cast my way at the show our first night there.

Indiana:

September rolled around, once again, and my anxiety level bumped up big time. As the evenings cooled, and the daylight hours grew shorter, so did my temper. Kara was back in school, but she worked with me in the evenings and on weekends. We were doing a bang up job in walk trot and she was looking forward to her first riding class at the CRHA National.

I complained to my brother, Frosty. "Its really getting cold, and Marcie has put our winter blankets on us already. Even the babies are wearing blankets."

"They must be going to the show with you."
Then he laughed as if something was tickling him. "What's so funny?" I asked him.

"You'll find out," he said. "We will probably be going to the boarding stable early this year. Could be as soon as you show gals get back."

"We never go this early," I told him.
"Sometimes, we do if the snow comes early and sticks around."

"That's all I need," I grumbled.
"Are you worried about the CRHA trip, Gunny?"
"Last year went pretty well, with the exception of our noisy arrival. I just can't shake the feeling that the curse is only beginning."

The countdown was on: the children increased their ride, and showmanship practice time.

Kelly could be heard yelling out to anyone who would listen. "Westward Ho!" He loved to travel and his exuberance was palpable. Kelly had his very own Rangerbred to show this year. Dumplyn was Millie's foal by my brother, Patch, I guess made her my niece.

George had been logging a lot of hours working with Dee Dee. She was another daughter by Patch, and out of a leased Quarter Horse mare. Dee Dee had a livered colored coat with a small star and frosting across her hips. She reminded me a bit of my mom, but Dumplyn was the mirror image of Millie. Both fillies were entered in the C.R.H.A. weanling filly futurity.

That evening while munching our evening hay, Frosty and I were going over the events of the day. I happened to remark, "Can you believe it, I'll have two babies traveling with me?" Frosty only gave me a big horselaugh. "Well, at least I'll have company on this trip," I commented as I turned my butt to him and ignored his continued laughter.

Our truck and trailer were old hat for me; it was the same rig that had brought me to my new home and family. My third outing to the annual CRHA pilgrimage took us west into Indiana. Like Northwestern Ohio, our destination was relatively flat. It had been easy for the babies to balance as we traveled the Turnpikes, Interstates, and winding country roads.

Thank the Great Horse in heaven we were on flat ground when the old blue truck, which now had a black bed instead of the original blue one, tried to die on us. George had mumbled something about rust eating the old bed just before he replaced it.

His comment confused me some. Our new neighbors had a horse named Rusty, and he had been known to eat almost anything he could wrap his teeth around, but I didn't think he could manage to chow down on a truck bed. Anyhow, our old blue truck was now black and blue.

I could hear Frosty's laughter echo between my ears when Dumplyn asked me, "Are we there yet?" for what seemed like the hundredth time. I guess you could call it payback for my driving her mom and Frosty crazy with the same question a few years in the past.

I was riding on the left, in Frosty's old spot. Dee Dee was on my right, and Dumplyn was in the stall behind mine.

"Hey, Gunny, what are those?" Dumplyn asked.

She had a better view of the scenery than I did, but I craned my head around to get a good look. I laughed at the bald white faces and heavy reddish brown bodies. "I think those critters are the cows that Cutter is always telling you tales about."

"Wow! They sure are funny looking.....BOOM! ...."What?" Dumplyn asked as the loud noise interrupted her comment on the appearance of the cows.

"I don' know," I told her. However, I knew the CRHA curse had struck again, but I kept that information behind my clamped lips. I didn't, want to frighten the little fillies. I was scared enough for all of us.

Out in the middle of nowhere our tow vehicle broke down. Whatever happened made a terrible noise that sent the cows in the pasture running in the opposite direction. I had fervently wished that we could have joined them in their flight to safety. I remember we had gradually rolled to a stop at the side of the road. At that point in our odyssey, the breeze that had come with forward motion and a bit of speed had been lost.

There we sat, on the side of a country road, sweltering in the afternoon sun. After what seemed like an eternity, we felt a jolt. We were moving again, but very slowly. Our slow motion journey brought us into a town with narrow streets and houses on either side of our trailer.

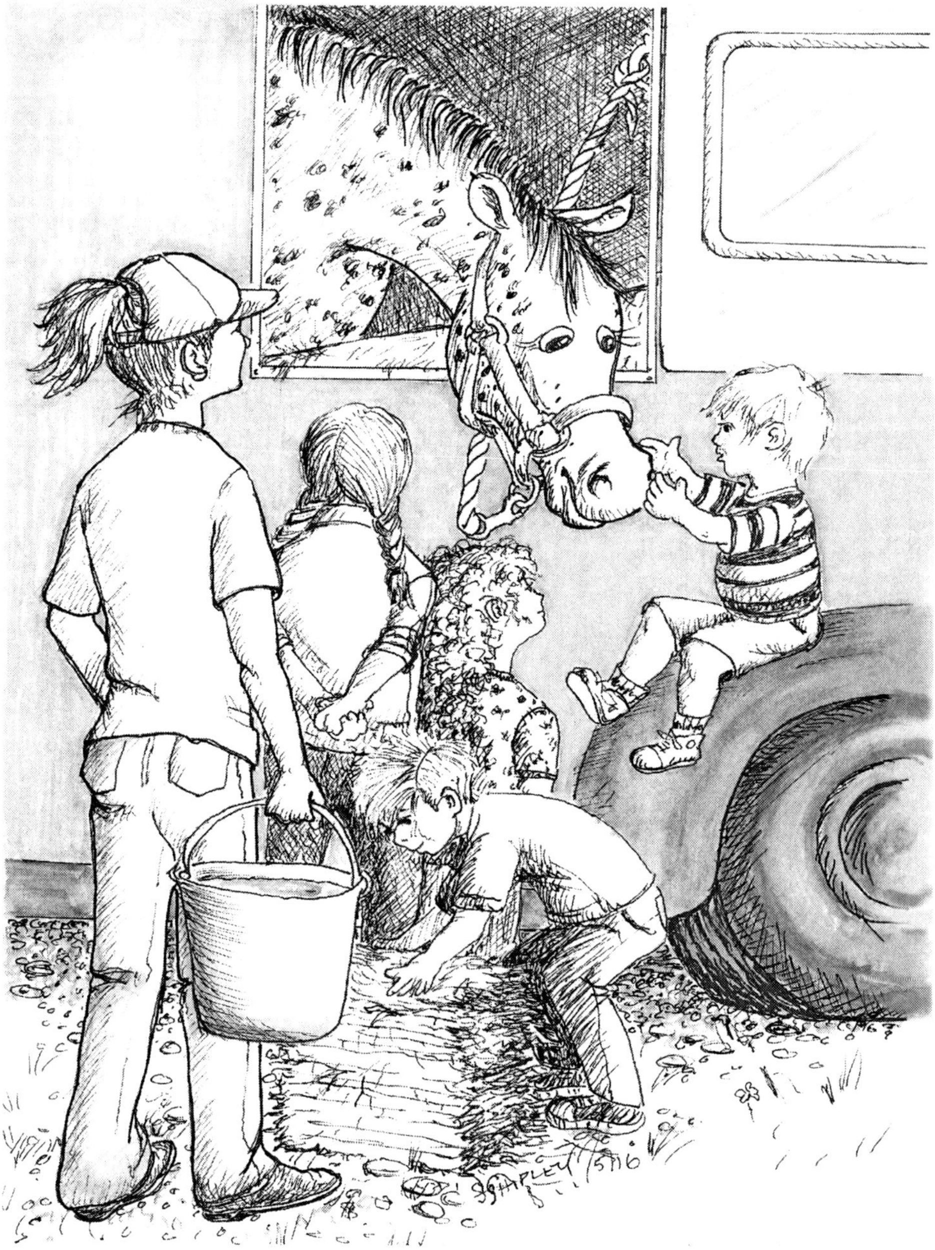

We finally rolled to a standstill. The stench of gas and grease was overpowering, and we all snorted in an attempt to clear our nostrils. I recognized the odors from previous trips when we stopped to give our tow vehicle a drink. That day our black and blue aging work vehicle was hauled away behind a larger truck with a big hook on it. Our trailer had been disconnected and we were alone. Well...not quite alone. Marcie and her children gave us some more hay and watered us again as they had done while we waited to get towed into town.

Every child in Smallville and their parents came by to peek at us. Some stood on the running boards to peer into our trailer, and a few parents lifted little ones to gawk at us. From her stall behind me Dumplyn had a better view of the thickening crowd. Those at the rear jostled for position to get a better look. "Gunny, are those people trying to get into our little stalls with us?"

She'd sounded worried, so I had tried to reassure her, "Don't fret, Dumplyn Marcie is standing watch, and she won't let anyone harm us." I glanced over to gauge Dee Dee's reaction, and she was dozing.

"They act like they have never seen a spotted horse before," Dumplyn commented.

I gave her observation some thought. My knowledge of humans was limited to horse-people, but I took a stab at an explanation. "It doesn't look like there are any places where a horse could live around here. Maybe the children have never seen any horse close up before."

Marcie answered a few questions, then chased the throng away, and gave us another cool drink.

Our truck made it through an operation to replace something called a universal joint. I have to admit that it sounded a lot healthier, but that repair stop took us into Indianapolis at dusk. We arrived several hours behind the rest of the Ohio group that we were to be stalled with.

Lights were already twinkling around the fairgrounds when Dumplyn was unloaded. She stood just taking in the strange sights and sounds. Then George backed Dee Dee out, and Marcie took my lead rope.

I stepped down and gave my usual greeting. "Hello! Is there anyone out there that I know?"

The first person to answer me was, Millie's daughter. "Me, Me, Dumplyn. You know me!" I snorted and rolled my eyes toward the great horse god. Then I heard a loud bellow.

"Hey, Love! It's me, Patch. Are the little ones with you?" I decided to pretend that I didn't hear him, but Dumplyn wanted to know who the horse with the deep voice, like Frosty's, was. That's my brother, Patch, and he is your sire." My explanation was barely given when she took over the lagging conversation.

She whinnied. "Hi, Daddy. This is Dumplyn." Patch welcomed her. Dee Dee remained silent and didn't seem to notice her new surroundings, which was very unusual for a filly only six months old. Marcie, Kara, and I led the parade to the designated stall area, followed closely by Kelly and Dumplyn. George leading his ever-silent charge brought up the rear. Once we were settled in and fed, the little ones took a nap. I quickly took advantage of the situation and stretched out for a snooze too.

Activities Saturday morning started with the futurity classes followed by the regular line up of halter and showmanship classes. Riding classes filled the remainder of the day. Dee Dee won the weanling filly futurity, and Dumplyn came in forth. The open weanling filly halter went much the same, but Dumplyn did a better job standing still for Kelly, and moved up a notch.

"Whoopee!" Kelly yelled as he waved his trophy and ribbon for showmanship, up over his head for all to see. His little spotted filly picked up on his excitement and danced at his side.

Patch's owner, Jessie, had brought a beautiful leopard colt to the show. Patch's son won the weanling stallion futurity class and his regular halter class. The colt also stood reserve champion in the junior stallion champion class. Our two fillies teamed up with Jessie's colt to win the Get of Sire class for Patch.

Marcie handled Dumplyn for that particular class, and it was the last time George would handle Dee Dee. She had been sold to a new family who lived in a place called California. But I digress: The show itself was a huge success.

Kara and I added to our growing collection of showmanship awards and I helped her win her first national trophy in walk trot. Also, on the bright side, Marcie's old nemesis didn't show up. It seemed he never cropped up when George and Marcie were close by, but I was beginning to think that he was stalking me.

Things began to change following our return from the Indiana National. Our old truck made it home without mishap, but it didn't survive the winter. Old black and blue went to the truck happy hunting grounds. It was replaced with a used red truck that sort of matched the red horse trailer. George picked up an old two-horse ride for Kara and me to travel to the 4-H shows while he put a new floor in the four horse. It got new fenders and a complete makeover. He could work on the restoration only a few hours during the week, and on the weekends when we weren't at a 4-H show.

I can't remember how long the two-horse trailer was my ride to events, but it was a bit cramped and I often rubbed off my tail wrap.

Kara had been really disappointed when her dad said there would not be a trip to the Nationals that year, but I was relieved.

The following September, Kara came down with a bug called the flu. I'm not sure what kind of bug that was, but one more year without the curse didn't disappoint me even a little.

George socked Marcie and the rest of us when he sold the old, red four-horse trailer after all the work he'd done on it. The red traveling rig became a part of history and was replaced by a silver truck and a matching four-horse gooseneck trailer. The new traveling accommodations gave our humans a place to sleep, change clothes, and even cook some meals.

At first, our new trailer seemed strange to me. We were accustomed to traveling with our muzzles pointed down the highway, but the stalls on the silver trailer were built on a slant. It sure was easier to maintain our balance on sharp turns or when a quick stop happened. We had a ramp to walk up, and windows in front of each stall that could be lowered on a hot day. This horse was ready to hop in and roll on down the road.

The next couple of years were pretty much uneventful, meaning no major disasters. We continued to travel the Appaloosa circuit. We frequented 4-H events and our county fair.

We went to some hunter meets, and a few hunter/jumper shows each year. Bigger hunter and dressage events were included after George brought home the new silver trailer.

As I look back, we didn't take another trip to the CRHA National Show until my eleventh year on this planet, and Kara was thirteen at that time. We had become an awesome team. Things were going along so smoothly that I nearly forgot about the curse.

The wreck of our new trailer prior to the planned trip to Pennsylvania for the National C.R.H.A. Show was a sad thing, but I was grateful the curse missed its aim and got only the trailer. George wasn't hurt, and none of us were on board when the trailer got mangled. I felt like kicking up my heels and doing a happy dance. We had one more year safe at home.

Pennsylvania:

Okay, you know how the humans say, *"Don't count your chickens until they hatch"*? Well, my relief at not going to the CRHA event that year was short lived, and I think that I finally figured out what the strange quote meant. My luck was about to run out.

Another Rangerbred lived in the southern part of our county, and his owner was friends with Marcie and George. So, guess who was invited to fill out the second stall in their trailer?

Some trailers I had to step up into, like the red trailer that had brought me to my new home; others had ramps to walk up. The two-horse that I'd been traveling around in during our summer jaunts had been equipped with a ramp as was our trashed silver trailer, and both were on easy inclines. My heart was racing so fast when I saw what was to be my ride to Pennsylvania that I feared it would pop out of me to land on the driveway. A truck was parked on the gravel surface, but there wasn't a trailer attached to it. Instead, a huge box sat where a truck bed usually was located. Marcie held me while George helped the lady driver lower the back of the box and open the stall doors. The sight of that steep ramp had me plotting an escape to the safety of my barn.

George was joking with Marcie when he said, *"We know Gunny can jump, but I think she will have to climb like a mountain goat to get in there."* George had a strange sense of humor, in my opinion.

"I'm not a mountain goat!" I whinnied.

A big, black gelding was already in the strange looking conveyance, and he nickered encouragement to me as I followed Marcie up the mountainous incline. A strange sense of foreboding raced along my spine when the heavy tailgate raised and slammed shut.

Three hours of bouncing down the road brought us to the show grounds. I had been over joyed to place my hooves on firm ground. Once more, I forgot my usual greeting. My legs began to move in a normal fashion as we moved up the aisle of a huge tent that housed portable stalls.

I got a good rest after our arrival on Friday afternoon because a brief rain hit the show grounds that evening. Kara and I worked a bit following breakfast the next morning. We were both cleaned up and ready for the morning halter and showmanship classes. Following a short break, it was time for our western classes. We were an awesome team that day and aced our western pleasure, horsemanship, reining, western riding, and trail classes. A note here, we were competing in the youth division of thirteen and under.

The schedule called for an auction following the last class of the day. Saturday concluded with a banquet that evening. My human family was in a building on the grounds having dinner while I munched on my hay. That was when the curse started to raise its ugly head. A couple of people stopped by my stall to look me over. I didn't pay much attention until I noticed one of the group was Bummer D. I backed into the farthest corner of my stall, laid my ears back, and tried for my ugliest face. I glared at him, and was restless the remainder of the night.

I kept my eyes open the next morning while Kara warmed me up for the hunter and jumper classes. The open hunter class went very well, and we won the class. We were waiting our turn to go into the open jumper class, and were walking and trotting around the show grounds to keep loose. That is when I spotted him again. Bummer D approached Marcie at the out gate of the show ring. I was too far away to hear the conversation, but it was evident by her body language that Marcie was not happy to see Sugar's old trainer.

Our exhibitor number was called as up next and we moved toward the in gate. I heard Marcie tell the folks with Bummer D, *"I'm sorry, folks, but Love is my daughter's youth horse and not for sale."* We entered the ring and Kara saluted the judge. My partner put me into a circle at a trot before approaching the first of ten jumps in the course. I wanted to get the event over with and get the heck out of Pennsylvania. I could feel his eyes tracking me. It was downright creepy. I sailed over the jumps in that course at nearly a full gallop. I came out edgy and snorting. It seemed, to me, it took forever for the others to complete the class. A jump pole down meant it had to be reset before the horse and rider could continue on the course. Most of the jumps had to be approached from both directions to accommodate the ten jumps of the course. Then came the lull for the places to be figured.

I had attempted to look pleasant for the photos with our trophy. Kara wanted a shot of us under the CRHA National Show banner with all our trophies and ribbons won at the show in the photo. It took a while to cart them to where the photo sessions were set up. Then she wanted her mom and dad in a photo with us.

It began to rain as we packed for the trip home. I was so ready to get out of that place that I was even looking forward to imitating a mountain goat. As it turned out, Marcie found me a ride with the barn boss from my winter boarding stable and her horse Beamer. I sure hope the curse doesn't break their trailer or truck.

A short while after we left the bumpy side roads and made the Interstate, the rains came down with a vengeance. Our trailer swayed several times during the increased pounding sound of the rain. It felt, to me, as if we slowed to a crawl. Then we stopped and our humans gave us some additional hay. Our humans offered us some water, the other mare drank, but I didn't like the smell of it and refused to quench my thirst.

My refusal to drink would soon have dire health consequences.

9
S.O.S!

Beamer and I were munching on hay while our human contingent chowed down in the truck stop restaurant while we waited out the storm. Marcie and Kara were in a building across the huge truck parking area from the place Beamer's owner had parked her rig and us.

My ears picked up the roar of another diesel as it pulled up next to us. Eighteen-wheelers had been coming and going, but there was something sinister about the sound of the one that had just pulled in. It remained on idle as the occupants of the truck stepped out into the rain. Strange voices mingled with the engine noise. Something was familiar about one of the voices, but before I could isolate the human sound from the raging storm the rear doors of the trailer were yanked open.

His stench assaulted my nostrils as soon as he stepped into the trailer. My heart raced as I sensed my peril. Beamer and I had been traveling on a slant with a vacant stall between us. We were in stalls two and four of a five horse trailer; centering our weight over the axles made the pull down the road better for the driver and the tow vehicle. I knew he was out to hurt me.

Beamer picked up on my distress and began to kick out a horse style SOS and screech for her owner. I appreciated her efforts, but wondered if anyone could hear us above the storm and the noise of the diesels. Marcie's nemesis unlatched the partition of the empty fifth stall, hooked it open, and then opened the divider that confined me. He had a lead rope in his hand. Was he under the impression that I was going peacefully? I let go with what Marcie called my rear guns. I don't think he had been expecting that sort of response from Kara's docile youth horse, but he had no idea about my barn name or how I earned it. As far as I was concerned, he was as much a predator as the coyotes Frosty and I had battled a decade earlier.

Bummer D was fast, and I only grazed him. *"Get the prod!"* He yelled to his accomplice. I had no idea what a prod was, but I was soon to find out. The other spooky person was dressed in a dark rain slicker. My stall window clanked in the wind when it was yanked open. Rain-slicker guy reached in with a long stick and shocked my chest. I backed up so quickly that I broke my halter and nearly plowed down Sugar's hateful ex-trainer, but he stood his ground long enough to stick me with a needle before retreating to close the trailer door.

I stood there shaking as the wind whipped rain poured through my window. Beamer continued whinny for help, but her vocal efforts were fading. Her urgent pleas began to sound farther and farther away as my head began to swim. That was the last thing I remember of trip back from Pennsylvania.

I recall that I awakened in a dark musty place. It was obvious I hadn't made it home from the PA National Show. I hadn't a clue where I was, but that cold scary place was a far cry from my home. I recall not having any idea how much time had passed. George, Marcie, and Kara must know that I'd been horsenapped, and I wondered if my human family was looking for me. I heard another horse in the darkness that surrounded me. "Hello" I nickered softly "Who else is here in this dungeon?"

"My name was Buddy, but this new batch of humans call me Jack-O."

We had several brief conversations that day, or night; it was so dark where we were it was hard to tell the time of day. I learned that Jack-O was a Thoroughbred with an impressive racing record he'd earned as a young horse. He told me that as he aged he was entered in a claiming-race where his current owner acquired him. His new human boarded him in this awful place during the off-season.

I will never forget the first time the huge barn doors creaked open. Bright rays of sunlight nearly blinded me, but wonderful fresh air came through too. A tall lanky silhouette materialized from the sunbeams. My eyes blinked him into focus as he approached to fill our water buckets and toss us some hay. Our benefactor was an adolescent boy with a shaggy mop of corn colored hair. So where was our grain? I was about to broach the subject with Jack-O when a big burly man took him out of the barn. I whinnied in distress. *"Don't worry, girl, Jack-O is only going out for some exercise. He'll be back,"* the young man told me.

The man who had taken Jack-O popped his head in the door. *"Frankie, put that spotted mare in the stud pen while you clean her stall."*

"Yes sir, Mr. Sutter."

"Frankie, watch out for her. I hear she is hell on the hoof."

I would bet to this day that my abductors spread those lies about me. However, if it had been Bummer D spreading the lies about my character, I did try to launch him into orbit. Frankie led me out to a cyclone fenced enclosure for the first time. In the daylight, I was able to get a better look at him. His eyes were the color of the summer sky, and he had as many freckles as I had spots. Walking the perimeter of my turnout area, I came to the conclusion there was not an escape from there. The stud pen reminded me of some dog kennels I had seen, but much bigger with sides taller than my head and a tented top.

I was on my best behavior so Frankie would continue to put me out when he did his chores. Things were going along peacefully for nearly a week, and then Bummer D showed his ugly face. Bummer and his creepy pals wouldn't enter my stall without first shooting me with a tranquilizer gun.

Time has absolutely no meaning when you are incarcerated in a dark prison. It seemed, to me, that I had been there forever. Depression overwhelmed me, and I fretted about never seeing my home, friends, or human family ever again.

After one of my encounters with the tranquilizer gun, I woke with itchy burning skin. Jack-O was the first to mention my new look. Mr. Sutter warned Frankie not to make an issue about my color. The few comments that reached my ears worried me. I figured I probably resembled Patch. Like Patch, my new color was liver chestnut. I retained my star and hind stockings, but my snowcap blanket had spots that Patch lacked. My mane and tail do-over had been a dark color that my horse companion couldn't determine in the dim light of the barn. "It looks black or a darker shade of your new coat." Jack-O commented. I wondered how my humans would find me when I didn't look like me?

Shortly after my makeover, grain had been reintroduced to my die. Not a total dummy, Bummer D paid Frankie to show me to prospective buyers. It was at one of these show and tell sessions that I learned more about my new look.

Frankie was cleaning me up for a buyer who was looking for a broodmare. *"It's not right, girl, to change you to look like another Appaloosa's papers. The poor mare is probably dead and some jerk sold her papers to your disreputable owner."*

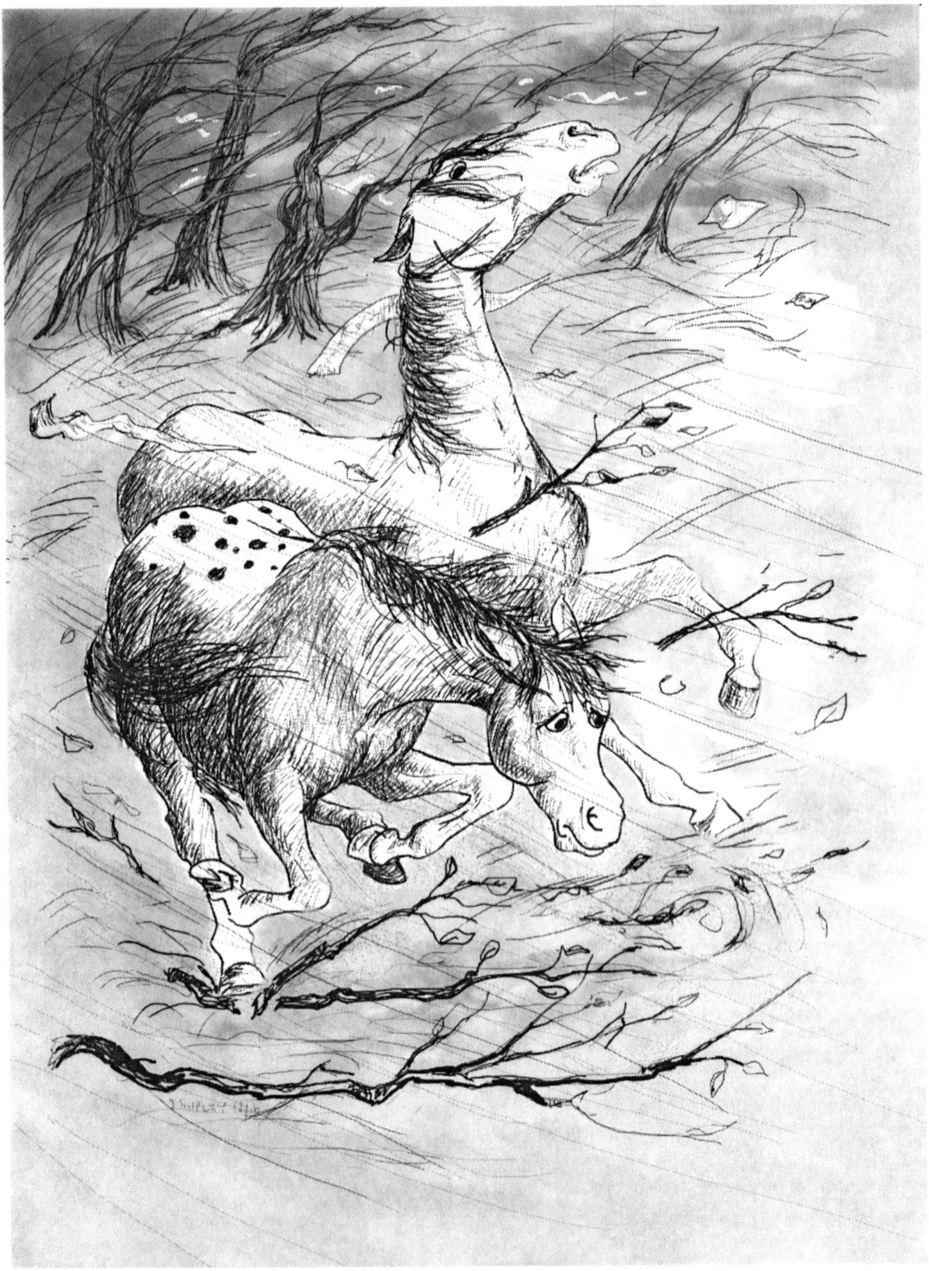

I only understood a few of his mumbled words, but his tone told me all I needed to know, and I was sure he wasn't talking about George or Marcie, I wondered who was claiming ownership to me.

Once more, my horse companion began to call for help. A monster storm splintered the huge wooden doors. A torrent of rain and hail blew through the opening, and we watched as lightning lit up the night on the heels of deafening thunderclaps. I wasn't waiting for human intervention. I backed up to my stall door and let go with what George referred to as my rear guns. My door shattered about the same moment that a lightning bolt ignited the hayloft in the old barn. Jack-O followed my lead and blasted through his door and we ran past the growing flames and into the stormy night.

We ran for our lives, but the storm was unrelenting and hail stung our hides. I had been in a few storms, but until then I had never seen cars sailing through the air or parking in trees. We were hit several times by flying tree limbs and other debris. If a safe place existed, neither of us was smart enough to figure it out. We just kept trying to run away from the roaring sound and the mayhem around us. When the storm finally ended, we were scraped, bloodied, and limping, but we'd survived.

Unfortunately, for me, Bummer D and his cohorts were the first humans to find us. They shot me with a tranquilizer, and I dropped off the edge of the world. I was patched up and shipped out. I never saw Jack-O again.

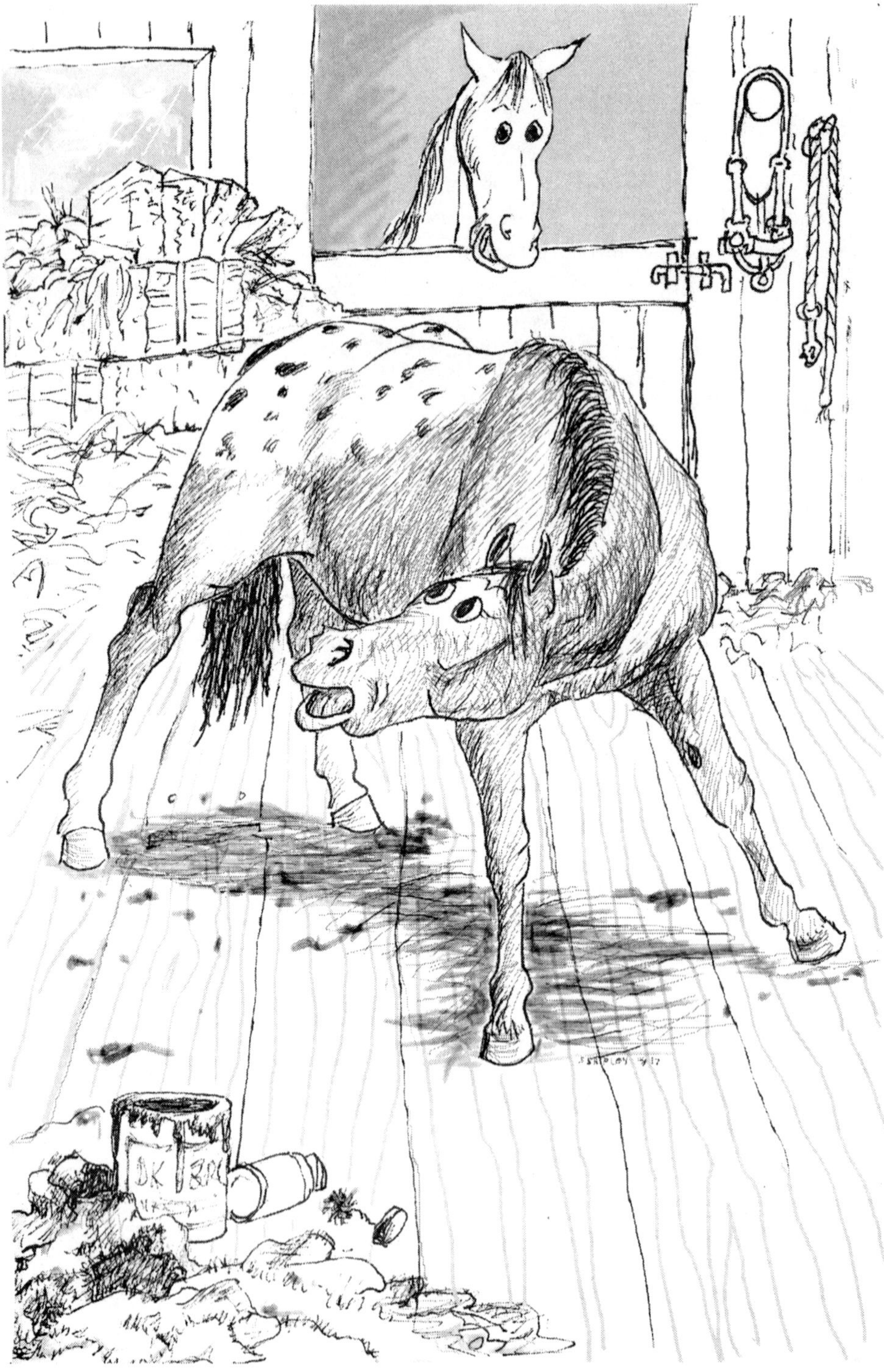

10
Shady Lady

As I look back on those dark years, time seemed to have progressed at a snail's pace. I was bit scarred up from the storm, and the potential buyer pool dried up. My abductors must have decided to cut their losses because they consigned me to an auction as a registered Appaloosa mare named Shady Lady. I was lucky to be purchased by a horse dealer who resold likely prospects to schooling stables or training facilities. Many of the other horses left on that sale for a trip south to the rendering plants in Mexico.

I ended up in a strange land with sand, hot sun, and not a speck of grass to be seen. My initial ride impressed the powers that be, and I was purchased as a school horse. Mr. Crump, the head trainer, was in the habit of assigning new horses to one of his assistants

Nancy was the assistant who was to work with me and access my abilities. She tacked me up with a hunt saddle and a ring snaffle. We traveled at a brisk ground-covering trot, and I cantered with gusto. It felt wonderful to be moving again.

A week or so later, I was stronger and working over cavaletti and crossbars. That routine was bumped up to a gymnastic course of ins and outs. I was working again and lost track of time, but soon I was popping over roll tops and four foot fences. My old training kicked in and I took the courses smoothly and on the correct lead whenever a change of direction was called for. I liked working with Nancy and we had developed some excellent chemistry.

Mr. Crump wanted to see me jump over some big fences, so he assigned me to Larry at the beginning of my second month. Four feet was the maximum of my experience as a hunter, and Larry was an aggressive rider who didn't try to get to know me.

Larry aimed me at the larger roll top, which had two poles above it, and when I refused to jump it, he hit me with the crop. He circled me around, spanked my butt, and dug in his puny English spurs as we approached take off. I galloped really fast and then executed a flawless sliding stop. I whinnied with delight as Larry sailed over the obstacle without me. I guess he didn't appreciate my solution to the problem of the bigger fence. He got back on and repeated the rump smacking as we approached the roll top again. I do believe he was expecting me to repeat my stop, but I rolled back one hundred and eighty degrees and kept on galloping. At that point, he yanked on my face, spanked my butt, and dug his spurs into my sides. I bucked him off and stood there glaring at him.

"That will do, Larry." Mr. Crump told him. Nancy walked me out, groomed me, and returned me to my stall.

Beginning the next day, Mr. Crump road me on the flat. Over the period of nearly a week he asked more and more of me. He assigned me to the dressage school where I helped him teach young riders the art of dressage.

I traveled to schooling shows where I took young and not so young dressage students into competition. As Lady S, I added to my string of wins for my riders. Of course no one knew of my previous accomplishments, which seemed to have happened in another life.

Lisa who was only ten and her grandmother, Mary, became my most frequent students and competition partners. They fell in love with me and leased me from Mr. Crump for their exclusive use. I have to admit that it was wonderful to have only two people riding me, and once more I had people who cared about me.

Lisa's dad surprised her and his mom, Mary, at Christmas. Rodger purchased Shady Lady as a joint gift since Mary had loved me enough to pay the lease on me for her and Lisa. I had discovered a week earlier that I was in a place in the Southwest called Arizona, and at Christmas I became part of the Brown family who lived there.

Rodger was a deputy sheriff in the county where they lived. He was part of the mounted patrol unit. The Brown Family lived a few miles out from a big city with a bird name that I can't remember. However, I do recall the concern in Roger's voice when he and Mary popped in for a visit one afternoon while Lisa was in school.

"Lady's coat color change is suspicious," Roger told his mom.

"Appaloosas frequently roan out," Mary assured him.

"I know, Mom, but horses usually change their coats much earlier in life. Lady's registration papers state that she is fourteen years old."

"Really, Rodger. Mr. Crump wouldn't do anything dishonest."

"Right, but what about Lady's previous owner?" he asked.

I gathered from their brief conversation and the way Roger kept ruffling my coat and inspecting my mane that I was shedding my disguise and becoming my old self.

As I continued to shuck off my dyed coat, I remained boarded at Mr. Crump's training stable while Lisa and Mary worked on their dressage skills. Two years passed as my riders and I progressed from schooling shows to sanctioned dressage competitions. Mr. Crump had long ago joined Roger in his opinion that something wasn't right with my registration description considering my drastic color shift.

Roger's patrol horse, Duncan, had been injured in the line of duty and was in need of a rest and some TLC. I'll give you one guess who got drafted. I went from a promising second level dressage horse to Rodger's replacement with the County Sheriff's Mounted Unit.

Lisa was a bit upset, but her dad placated her by promising to have Mr. Crump look for another dressage horse for her. He also told her that I could come back as soon as Duncan was well enough to return. Lisa made it her mission to take over Duncan's care and rehab.

Horse orientation for the mounted units was a bit bizarre and required nerves of steel. Occasionally, the old monsters that had haunted the arena during my early years would rear their ugly heads.

Lights flashing on the top of cars didn't bother me much, but the ear splitting shriek of the sirens was another story all together. Sirens and the gunfire turned my nerves of steel to mush. I got a handle on the siren issue long before I could muster a stoic response to Roger's gun going off while he was on my back. The pop of my rider's gun brought back memories of the tranquilizer gun, and I had expected to drop in my tracks.

Most of the trail obstacles had been conquered in my previous life, so the rocking bridge was not a big deal; however, the demon training course designer added a car wash test. I was a little hesitant about walking through the wide rubber looking strips that hung from a rail high above my head, but I had developed a trust of Roger so I walked forward. Okay the strips didn't harm me, but once in there I encountered another set of strips to negotiate to get us out. I was boxed in. A shower of water hit us before I could exit the other side. I'd become more reluctant the second time we practiced the car wash. After a dozen more tries I passed the test. However, I aced most of my trials on the first or second attempt, and I figured the rest of this police horse training was going to be a piece of carrot cake.

11
Spotted Patrol

I'd been paired up with several veteran police horses during my apprenticeship. We trailered to the far reaches of the county. We searched for lost children, a few burglars, and even scoured an area near a ranch where a rancher had reported seeing a UFO. I really didn't know what that was, but the owner said the aliens took three of his steers. We never found anything to explain the disappearance of his cattle.

Another outing put me in the company of a group of seasoned patrol horses, and we were assigned to cover the county fair for the week. Fairs were old hat for me, and patrolling the parking area and the livestock areas went pretty well. Our officers and horses worked in shifts. I had been assigned the early morning my first couple of days, and our shift usually ended about the time the evening rush began.

Midweek, Roger and I along with two other teams went up the midway to check out reports of a ruckus near the kiddy rides. I was marching up the midway, the one place that 4-H horses hadn't been allowed. I have to admit that I had been a bit apprehensive, but I didn't want to screw up in front of the other two horses. The whole episode started when one of the fellows working a ride challenged the wristband day passes worn by two preschoolers. He had snagged each child by the arm at the ride exit. His supposed purpose was to take the children to the front office to verify their passes. Watchful parents were in hot pursuit. Mom pulled her children from the offender's grasp, and Dad decked the guy trying to walk off with his little son and daughter.

A pair of city police officers carted the fellow with a broken nose off in a black and white, and we returned to patrolling the grounds. That was the most exciting thing that happened that week.

As I became more accomplished, I graduated from rural searches to city streets for special events. Most were peaceful, and I was a big hit with the city kids. They all wanted to touch the spotted patrol horse. One event that remains vivid for me was working the crowd at a political rally in a shopping strip.

Part of my initial training had been to stand my ground with gunfire around me. Well…that day some deranged person decided to take out a congress person and several of those gathered including a ten-year-old girl. The amount of gunfire that day and the cries of those who had been shot will remain with me until my last breath. Fortunately, most of my years with the mounted unit were relatively peaceful.

Our patrol was off to compete against other mounted units from around the United States and Canada. I got sidelined on that trip, and Duncan went instead. It seemed the other members of the patrol thought I ruined the cohesive appearance of the unit. I guess what Kara used to call plain brown wrappers had a decided advantage in the drill team part of the competition.

Lisa had a new mount for dressage competition. His show name was Doctor Love, and the name struck my funny bone. Not so funny was being pushed aside as Roger's patrol horse. Duncan came through with flying colors at the competition and was reinstated to active duty upon the units return home,
Mary took advantage of my availability and we began to accompany Lisa and the rest of Mr. Crump's group to dressage shows around the country.

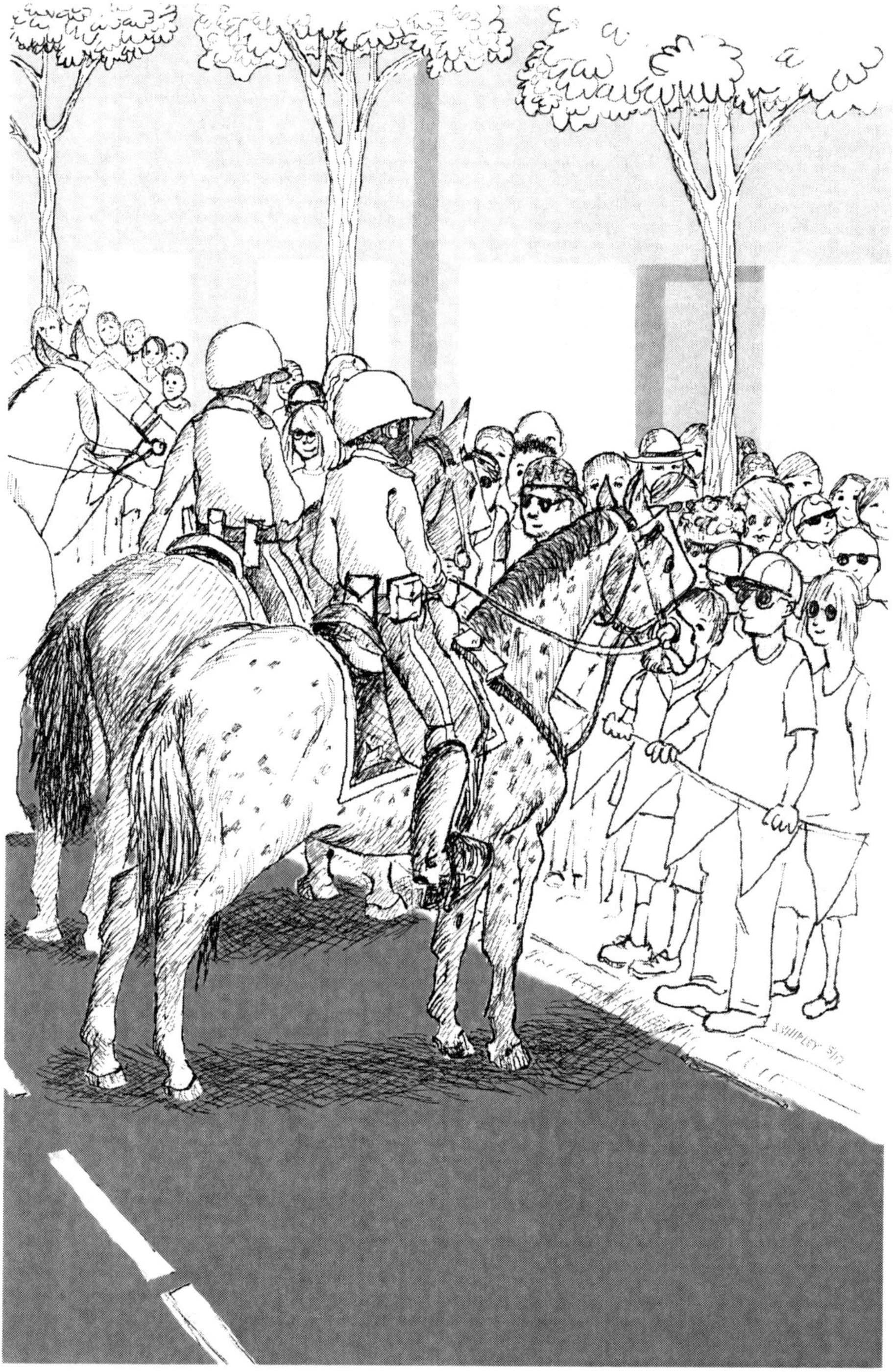

Several years passed while Mary and I perfected our dressage tests. It had become commonplace for her to refuse a reader for our competitive rides. Mary had a fantastic memory and she found the readers used by most of our competition more distracting than helpful. We covered old ground using training level tests and were making a statement in our first level tests. Mary and I along with Lisa and Doctor Love, joined with five other top ranked horse and rider teams to hit some major dressage events during 2005 and 2006.

June of 2007 found us at the Lake Erie Dressage Derby. I had gotten used to the journalists and spectators questioning Mary and taking photos of us. At Mr. Crump's urging, Mary had joined several State and Regional dressage clubs. Her joining a club in Northern Ohio turned out to be the catalyst for another shake up in my life.

The Northern Ohio Club hosted the Lake Erie event, and held special yearend Century Combination award division. I discovered we were the leading horse and rider team. Awards in the Century Combination division were given to the horse and rider whose combined age equaled at least one hundred years. Though I found it hard to believe, my papers said I was twenty-eight years old, and Mary had seventy-five years under her belt.

We had been busy with post show interviews and a photo shoot when a local trainer approached Mary.

She introduced herself and then asked, *"How did you come to own Gunny, Mrs. Brown?"*

"I'm sorry, but you're mistaken. My horse's name is Shady Lady" Mary told her.

Carrie Sanders clarified her question. *"Your mare looks remarkably similar to a mare a friend of mine used to own. Gunny was her nickname. She was registered as Chelsea Love.*

"I purchased Lady from Mr. Crump eight or nine years ago."

"Thank you for taking the time to talk with me, Mary. Lady is a lovely horse and I'm sure her resemblance to Chelsea Love is only a coincidence. I wish you well with the rest of the season." With that backhanded comment, Carrie Aanders disappeared into the throng surrounding us.

I had been hamming it up for the photographers and reporters covering the event. Folks with video cameras and cell phones were also among our fans. A few even wanted to take selfies with us. Then, I heard my name old name mentioned by the woman named Carrie. My ears perked up, and I turned my head to get a better view of the person speaking to Mary. I hadn't heard my registered name since I left the C.R.H.A. National in what seemed like a universe away, and in another lifetime.

We made a couple of side trips to smaller dressage events on our return to Arizona. I had forgotten about the brief encounter with my old name by the time we returned home. Mary was unable to shake the encounter with my old identity, and she was more inclined to rethink Roger's initial reaction to my drastic color change.

12
A Long Road Home

We'd been home only a few days when Mary, Roger, and Mr. Crump all popped in at the same time to visit with me. It had been a strange visit. The three of them stood in the aisle way peeking in at me and then down at a piece of paper in Roger's hand.

"*Lady sure looks like the horse in this old reward flyer,*" Roger commented.

Mr. Crump shook his head as he gazed at me. "*It makes more sense in hindsight that a horse with Lady's level of training could end up at an auction frequented by renderers.*"

"*Well, whatever the original plan was in abducting this mare was, something caused the thief or thieves to try to unload her while she resembled the description on Shady Lady's registration certificate,*" Roger Speculated.

The following morning the vet showed up to draw my blood and pull a few of my mane hairs out by the roots for something called a DNA report. I had blood drawn for one test or another throughout my life, but I don't recall ever having my mane pulled out for any reason. Once the vet left, Mary told me she'd say a prayer that the tests matched the papers for Shady Lady.

We'd been back a bit shy of two weeks, by Mary's reckoning, when we were visited by a couple of people from my past. It took me by surprise that Marcie and George had also roaned out since our last time together. They both had gray hair now, but I would have known them anywhere. I didn't have a clue how much time had gone by on the human calendar since I'd been horsenapped. Then, I overheard Marcie's conversation with Roger.

"*Gunny was abducted when she was eleven. She was registered in 1977 as Chelsea Love, which makes her thirty this year. We never thought we would ever see her again,*" Marcie said.

It was hard to tell who wore the more ominous scowl, Roger or George. They were in deep conversation as they walked from the barn and left me to try to sort out their next moves. I wondered if I would have to leave my new family and return with Marcie and George.

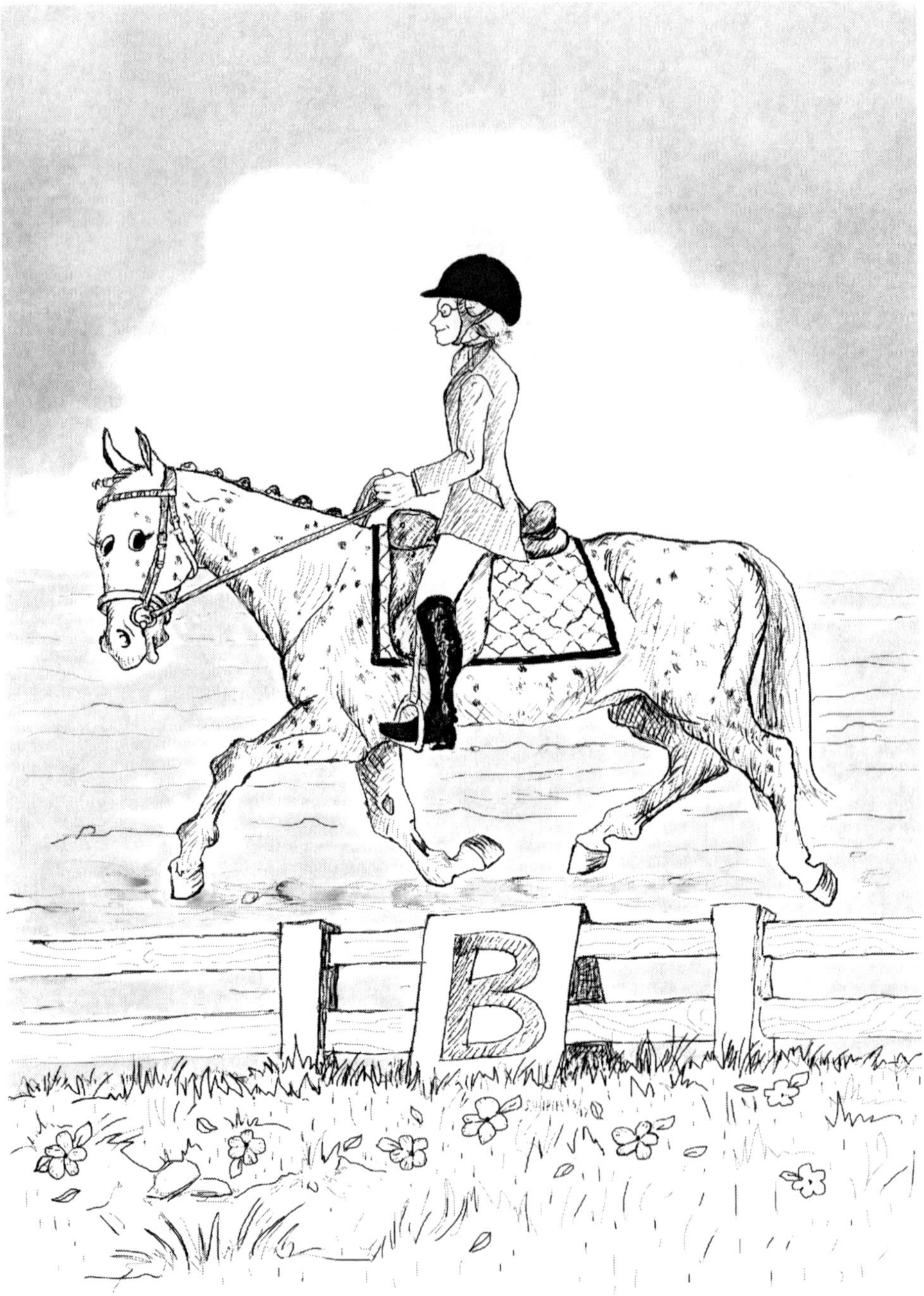
B

Marcie and George visited for a couple of days before they flew home and left me behind. All my fretting about where my loyalties should be had been settled by the humans, as usual.

The Appaloosa Horse Club finally notified Mary of the DNA results. Roger was livid. It appeared that the Quarter Horse mare and the Appaloosa stallion used to produce Shady Lady didn't match my DNA. Mary was heartbroken when the results arrived. As it turned out Shady Lady had been two years younger than me.

Roger gave me a juicy red apple while he talked to me. *"Well, girl, it looks like you aren't such a Shady Lady after all. Don't worry, we'll get the culprits who took you away from your old home."*

My human families, past and present decided I should remain where I was. Roger told me that I was to stay undercover as Shady Lady until they tracked down Lady's previous owner's. I wondered if Roger and other law officers would be able to track down Bummer D and his nasty cohorts. I hoped they could find them and disrupt their illicit enterprise before another horse fell victim to their evil ways.

Mary and I picked up our riding routine, but she kept our outings limited to schooling shows in the Southwest. I think she gave me silly commands every now and then, so we wouldn't win too much and could fit in better with the level of the other riders. Fitting had been a little tricky considering my spotted coat, which always drew stares and a good many comments. Truthfully, the ease up in the level of our rides turned out to be a good thing, for me. My old hip and hock injuries from the storm that Jack-O and I had been caught in started to bother me more and more over the last couple years.

Mary took to riding me around the farm at a sedate walk and trot as my arthritis intensified and lameness kept us from the dressage ring. She lavished me with attention and yummy treats. I think that she knew our time together was growing short.

Two more years passed since Mary and I had tripped in to my past life at the Lake Erie Dressage Derby. Roger's initiating an investigation netted the arrest of several of Bummer D's cohorts. However, Sugar's old trainer had been found several years earlier trampled in the stall of a wild-eyed stallion. Bummer D's fate had been shared with police when the rest of horse theft ring had been rounded up. I figured he probably abused the horse one too many times.

I had nearly put Bummer D out of my mind. I must have been getting forgetful in my old age, but I could finally let him go. He was probably in a very hot place and being punished for his evil ways.

Not long after the news circulated about the horsenappers, Marcie and George showed up again. This time they brought a horse trailer with them. They visited for a few days, and then I began my long ride back to the home of my youth.

13
More Lazy Summer Days

My heart swelled with joy as I once more stepped from the horse trailer on to the turf of my youth. The sweet scent of lilacs in bloom filled my nostrils, and the spring grass tickled my ankles as I followed Marcie across the paddock. My old stall felt like horse heaven. Dumplyn greeted me while Marcie removed my halter.

"About time you got home, Love," she snorted.

What could I say? I wanted to forget the nightmare that followed our last C.R.H.A. National Show, and it was the last thing I wanted to discuss. "I got lost," I told her and then went to munching my hay. Several hours had passed and George as well as Marcie came to check on me, I asked Dumplyn why Kara didn't come to visit with me.

My heart sank in the direction of my hay filled tummy when she told me, "Kara doesn't live here anymore."

It had crossed my mind that my person was mad at me for being away for so long, but it never occurred to me that she was gone. "Will she be returning? I asked my niece.

"She comes back on human holidays, something called spring break, and she spends the summer with us. Marcie says she is away at school."

I always peeked out my window whenever I returned from a lengthy pasture tour, but Kara was nowhere to be seen. Dark shadowy figures reached for me whenever I dozed off. Dumplyn speculated that they were only left over spooks from my recent past, but they felt real to me. Perhaps home was the dream and I would awaken in that damp cold place absent of sunlight.

I lost my appetite when the days darkened, thunder rolled, lightning split trees, and shook the ground. As quick as the bolts from the sky, I flashed back to the lightning strike that lit up that musty prison from where I'd run for my life. My weather blues continued for three days. The sun came back the afternoon of the fourth day, and so did Kara.

She buried her face in my mane and wept. *"Oh, Gunny, I thought I would never see you again. It seems like forever."*

My sentiments exactly! I nuzzled her shoulder and much of the darkness that haunted me was magically lifted. It was probably too much to hope that those specters would completely dissolve, but I also had the happier years with my family in Arizona to remember, and those good memories sure helped.

Kara and I rode around the farm and it was much as I remembered it. Trees seemed taller and much of the fences had been replaced. I found out that she had been away at school for nearly a decade and was working on something called a dissertation for a PhD.

George groomed me and rode me around the farm several times a week while Kara was away at what she called a university. George rode Dumplyn when he and Marcie went trail riding. Dumplyn and I were the last Appaloosas left on the farm. The younger horses were all Quarter Horses, with the exception of one little Haflinger filly.

Kara came home several times during the year, but spring break was a special event. She brought the light back into my life and chased away the dark places that had threatened to engulf me. It is good to be home. Maybe Toy was correct and the great horse spirits were watching over me during the dark days of my life, and brought me home. The horse god had also rewarded me with my Arizona family.

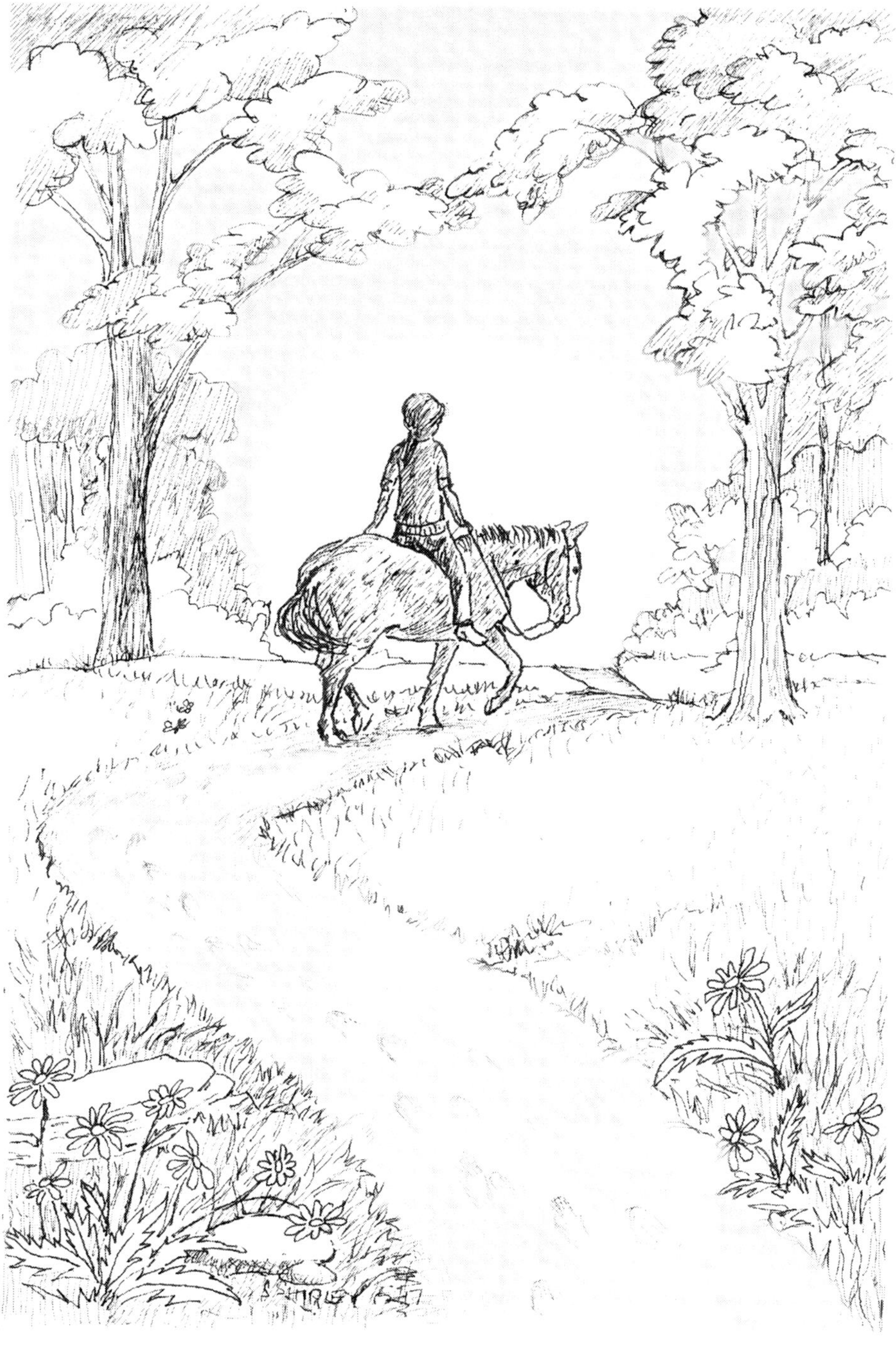

Dumplyn and I spend a lot of time remembering the old days with Frosty, Cutter, Kid-O, and her mom, Millie. It's hard to believe Dumplyn is twenty-seven, and I am thirty-three. Sometimes she joins me for a nap under the huge sycamore tree. I take a lot of naps there, and sometimes I think I hear Frosty.

"About time you got home kid. See yah soon, Gunny."

APPENDIX

RANGERBRED FACTS

The Rangerbred horse is registered with the COLORADO RANGER HORSE ASSOCIATION INC.-the oldest of the western horse breed registries still in existence in the United States.

To meet the requirements for registration with the CRHA, a horse MUST SHOW A DIRECT DESCENT from one of the two foundation stallions, MAX #2 and/or PATCHES #1.

The CRHA is NOT A COLOR REGISTRY. The founder wisely decided that a horse's ability has not a thing to do with his hide. Because of this, Rangerbreds come in a wide variety of color patterns: from solid bays and chestnuts, classic blacks, grays and roans, all the way to colorful blankets and vivid tri-color leopards.

The Rangerbred may be outcrossed on horses of other breed registries including, The American Jockey Club, The American Quarter Horse Assoc., The Appaloosa Horse Club (USA, Canada & Foreign), The Arabian Horse Club, ARA-APP and the ICAA (with certain reservations). The outcrossed mare must be registered with one of the above registries or show positive proof of parentage tracing to one of the registries accepted or a combination of the above registries (with approval). There is a hardship clause for geldings and spayed mares only.

The cornerstone for the Rangerbred horse was laid in 1878 when General U.S. Grant, during a world tour, visited Sultan Abdul Hamid of Turkey.

As a token of deep friendship, the old Sultan presented the General with two desert stallions on the day of his departure. One was an Arabian named Leopard, the other a Barb named Linden Tree (Both of these stallions are listed in the studbooks of two American breed registries, The Arabian Horse Club and the American Jockey Club. Their impact on the horse world touches almost every breed in the United States today.)

The next person of note in the evolution of the Rangerbred horse was a man by the name of Mike Ruby. He was born in Tavastock, Ontario, in 1886, and emigrated with his parents to the eastern Colorado plains at the age of three. It was the era of the cattle barons and good using horses were in great demand. The Rubys were noted horsemen, and Mike took an early interest in the superior horses being bred on the Whipple ranch. The Whipples were carrying on an intensive line-breeding program with Barb-Arab seed stock, which they had obtained from the General Colby ranch in Beatrice, Nebraska. These horses had a reputation of working ability, good dispositions, and plenty of stamina.

In the early 1930's Mike Ruby acquired Patches, a son of the stallion from the Colby Ranch (Tony), and Max, a halo-spotted son of the Waldron Leopard out of an Arabian mare, as his herd sires. By this time he had amassed a herd of more than 300 mares! With these two foundation sires, Mike began to build the breed. Both Stallions left outstanding sons who went into the Ruby herd as sires. Of prime importance among these were Patches II, Leopard and Ranger who, as well as their own sires, figure in the pedigrees of most present day Rangerbreds.

Mr. Ruby was different in many ways than many of the ranchers of his day...before most of the prominent registries were founded...., as he maintained accurate written records of his mares, stallions, and their offspring. At this time, these records including foaling dates, colors, and their complete pedigrees was indeed an unusual practice. These handwritten records have been preserved as a part of the CRHA Corporate records.

In 1934, Mr. Ruby was invited to display two of his stallions at the Denver Stock Show. The two leopard patterned stallions (Leopard #3 and Fox #10) were seen by thousands of visitors. Encouraged by the faculty of what is now Colorado State University, the new breed of horse was officially named Colorado Rangers, horses originating in Colorado and bred and raised under range conditions. Verbal references to those "range bred" horses eventually led to their being more commonly known as Rangerbreds, although the official name remains.

With the naming of the breed came a breed registry. **Mike Ruby founded the Colorado Ranger Horse Association in 1935.**
Two years later he applied to the State of Colorado for corporate charter, which was granted on January 4th, 1938. Due to registration only being available to CRHA members and a fifty-member limit imposed, many horses with Rangerbred heritage were not able to be registered with CRHA at that time. Those horses with color patterns, however, were gladly accepted by another breed registry that came into being several months later, **The Appaloosa Horse Club.** Mr. Ruby dedicated his life to the building of a new American breed, and served as president of the Colorado Ranger Horse Association until his death in 1942.

In 1964, the Colorado Ranger Horse Association lifted the fifty-member limit and registration was opened up to all horses meeting the pedigree requirements, regardless of owner membership status. Since then, the CRHA has registered many of the Appaloosas with Rangerbred heritage that were "lost" to the organization for so many years.

Additional Appaloosa bloodlines with Rangerbred connections are still being recognized through continued pedigree research. Most recent research indicates that one out of every eight Appaloosas is eligible for CRHA registry. Appaloosa pedigrees are checked for Rangerbred heritage by the organization at no charge to the horse owner.

(C.R.H.A History excerpts were selected from the breed website. For additional information and complete story go to http://www.coloradoranger.com/history.html)

AUTHOR NOTES

Dear reader,

Thank you for choosing this book.

I hope you enjoyed "Don't Call Me Love" and will take a moment to review her tale. The Backyard Horse Tales equine stars' personalities were borrowed from special horses that have graced my life at one time or another.

If you would like to know more about me, or the horses that inspire these tales, stop by for a visit at http://talesbyjackie.com.

The following piece was written, for my blog, when I was struggling with "Frosty and the Nightstalker." I think you may appreciate this more than additional blah, blah, blah about me.

Jackie

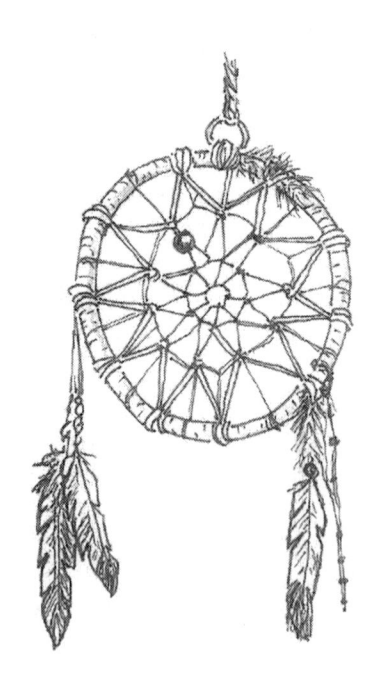

SPIRITS THAT PROWL THE NIGHT

Characters in a story can, and often do haunt an author's sleep. A writing coach of mine once told me, "Keep a note book beside your bed, and one in your pocket. You never know when inspiration will strike." I wish I could tell you I adhere to that advise, but I seldom do.

In the predawn hours of a July morning, in 2012, Frosty paid me a visit. The twenty-six years that Frosty lived among us he occasionally escaped the confines of his stall. His night wanderings always seemed to take place at strange hours. His mission appeared to be to scare the bejesus out of me. I often wonder why I wasn't gray by my mid-thirties. You would think by that night I would have been used to his night prowling and visits. However, Frosty passed on to horse heaven twenty-one years prior to this early morning visit.

I have tried to rationalize those hours before dawn broke; so for the sake of sanity, we will assume that I was dreaming. The following dialog is the conversation as best as I can recall. In my stories the horses narrate the events in their lives, but they never talk to people.

Something woke me, and I tried to assess the reason my heart was racing. July always makes me nervous. The month brings a loft full of fresh hay, neighbors with celebratory fireworks, and random thunderstorms. Fire is the worst of my fears for my beloved horses, Trapped in their stalls they quickly become panicked. Often, horses rescued from a burning barn will run back into their stalls where they feel safe.

The sky was clear, and every star was visible as I rolled over to blink the roof of the horse barn into view, Everything seemed peaceful. The horses wouldn't begin to demand their breakfast for several hours, but I couldn't relax.

I felt someone in the darkness moving closer, and then the darkness of night faded to show the shadowy form of a horse. I recognized him immediately. "Frosty, what are you doing here?"

I gave myself a mental reprimand, for my squeaky response, and hoped that I hadn't roused the rest of the household. His form began to solidify. He stood before me—at the foot of my bed—not the aged horse that had passed on, but my beautiful Appaloosa in his prime. Then, he spoke to me!

"Howdy Jack. I heard you call me, so I stopped by to see if I could help."

His verbalization threw me. It was true, I had been thinking about him a lot at the time as I worked on his tale. I wondered if I had, indeed, called out to him during my restless night. Okay, I thought, I should take advantage of the opportunity to speak with him, "Do you know about the book I'm working on that includes you?"

"Oh yeah, I know. Sox, thinks it's funny that you didn't have much trouble with his story, and Love is making me crazy! She wants my book out of the way, so you can finish her memoirs."

I laughed at his descriptions of the other two horses; it fit their unique personalities perfectly. He tossed his beautiful head, before snorting at me in a disgusted manner. My sense of humor escaped him, so I explained while struggling to make my voice soft and serious. "Your tale is more complicated, and took a lot of research. Then it was a challenge weaving the historical facts into a horse's point of view. Most of it is complete and I am working with an editor to make sure the story flows, and is interesting for our young readers."

"You know, Jack, I wasn't so sure about the whole reincarnation theory at first. Now you've started down that path you need to finish."

"I know. I've talked to Kellie and Pat about the ending. I discussed it at length with Sandy, our illustrator, about the best way to handle the whole issue that isn't too dark for our youngest readers." He stood there like the patient old soul he had always been. I believe he was waiting to see what more I could contribute. My brain still wasn't firing on all cylinders. I answered his questioning gaze with a shrug of my shoulders, as my eyes tried to drink in the sight of him.

He glanced over his shoulder into the early dawn. "Well, if my opinion carries any weight, I agree with Kellie. Just do it! It is the only way I can exist in my part of the story, but I still think the story is a little spooky. On the other hoof, I like the idea of sharing a bit of Appaloosa history with people." Once more, he looked toward the east and the rising sun. "It's time for me to go."

It hit me that I was losing him once more. I whiped my eye leaks with the bed sheet that had fallen to my lap as I bolted to a sitting position when he first spoke. "Frosty, say hello to the others for me."

I will. Bye, Jack."

Poof! He just faded away, and I went to frantically writing before the dream vanished. Frosty's visit gave me the answer for how I was to approach the climax of his story. I sure hope he likes the results. It is kind of hard to tell about Frosty, he had always been such a stoic individual. Nothing much ever bothered him. The one exception to his bravery had been his dread of crossing rivers. It was his out of character fear of water that gave me the idea for Backyard Horse Tales 2; "Frosty and the Nightstalker."

I sure hope Love doesn't decide to show up to prod me along with her story. You know how mares are, and Love was a terror at certain times. Wow! Talk about PMS. We used to butt heads in her early training. Maybe Frosty was really an old soul that came to earth to teach me the patience required to make child-safe mounts out of some of the horses to follow him that never quite filled his hoof prints.

Meet the Illustrator

My earliest recollections include animals, any and all animals, but especially horses. As soon as I could hold a pencil, I was drawing them. To me there was and is nothing so beautiful or smells so good as a horse.

Years of shameless begging wore my parents down and when I was 14 they bought me my first horse. His name was Rex, he was a bay Saddlebred and he was my heart for the next 22 years. Many a teenage tear was cried into his mane and many happy hours were spent riding, grooming and stall cleaning. About the same time Rex came into my life, I began taking private art lessons as well as art classes in school. After graduation, I attended a commercial art school. During this time I earned a modest living painting portraits, mostly horses and dogs, but a few of humans also.

To round out my life, I broke a few horses, was a 4H advisor and taught horsemanship and riding. In the ensuing years I worked at a number of jobs to support myself and my son. When an especially lucrative job moved to North Carolina, I went to work for Valley Tack Shop as a salesperson, buyer, artist and saddle fitter, where I still work to this day. It was here that I first met Jackie Anton then a customer at the shop. Jackie eventually wrote and published her first book, "Backyard Horse Tales 1, Sox". Since I am the book buyer at Valley, she asked if I would consider stocking the book in the shop.

I was more than willing. This led to conversations concerning her next book and happy day, she asked me to illustrate it.

Once again I was more than willing! This was the realization of a lifelong dream to illustrate a book! It was about a horse, how perfect. That book was "Backyard Horse Tales 2, Frosty and the Nightstalker. Now here we are, sending forth the next book Jackie wrote, "Backyard Horse Tales 3, Don't Call Me Love". This has been a learning process for me, exciting and fulfilling. I am and always will be grateful to Jackie for being the wonderful writer, employer, corroborator and friend that she is.

Sandy Shipley

More art by Sandy Shipley
ship1941@sbcglobal.net

Excerpt from Backyard Horse Tales Sox 2nd edition

Chapter 1
A New World

It had been a long voyage, eleven months exactly, getting to here from there. My assigned quarters were comfortable, and all my needs had been seen to, but I could not wait to explore the new world. Maybe I had cabin fever, I was becoming very uncomfortable, and my traveling capsule seemed to have shrunk. At the beginning of my voyage there had been plenty of room for me to move around, but now I felt restrained. Close to my final destination, I began to have doubts that I would make a successful landing. My environmental suit had just sprung a huge leak, and it collapsed around me.

I put my foot through the escape hatch, and I encountered icy air. The blast of frigid air changed my mind about putting my footprints on this planet, and I decided to stay inside where I was warm and safe. I tried to pull my foot back in, but an unknown force was pushing on my backside as it guided me toward the escape hatch. Help! My left foot dangled out there, and the pressure from behind was getting stronger, but my right foot was stuck. I struggled to move it in line with my left leg, but it didn't want to cooperate. Finally I succeeded in placing my legs in a good position to land. I stretched my neck, put my nose between my front legs and that was when I tumbled out onto the hard prickly surface of an alien environment. The hard landing did not tear the collapsed suit from my face, and I was too tired to struggle with it.

It had been hard work getting into this strange new world. Exhaustion had taken the edge off of my long awaited arrival, and breathing in this atmosphere was proving to be impossible.

A soft nickering sound from my mother reassured me, but her voice sounded different in this new world. At first I thought I heard other voices nicker a welcome, but their voices too were fading. My head was spinning and I began feeling very weak. Part of my protective suit was now blocking any air supply. The lifeline that had attached me to my mother had broken when I fell to earth. The remains of the umbilical cord that provided nourishment and oxygen during my long journey dangled from my tummy.

An alien sound tickled my ears, a whisper. *There is the foal, it is lying against the stall door. Open the door carefully, Bill, and pull the placenta away from the baby's nostrils, so that it can breathe.*

Strong appendages gently removed the covering from my nose, and I took my first deep breath; relief flooded through me. While I tried to recharge from my near death experience, I heard a grunt; it was my mother. She had been resting in the deep straw too. She was very tired and weak after helping me into this world. Soon she rose to her feet and came close to me. Mom began pushing me to stand up too.

She nuzzled and encouraged me, "Come on, son, on your feet."

Easy for her to say, she was already an old pro at standing, but I was having trouble untangling my long gangly legs. Instinct and constant encouragement from Mom made me try again. I gathered my back legs under me and shoved.

"OOPS! Not quite so hard, son." Mother cautioned me, as I tumbled onto my side. "It would probably help, son, to uncross your front legs first. Try again."

Three tries later, I succeeded. The effort was sure worth it! Mom guided me back along her large warm body, until I found her fresh supply of sweet milk. It warmed my belly and it made me feel stronger.

I plopped down for a nap once my tummy was full, and that was when the front wall opened. A chilly gust of cold air ushered strange two-legged creatures into my world. The two of them came in through an opening that had appeared in the wall, as if by magic. I tried to get a good look at them, but everything was fuzzy. The larger of the creatures knelt down beside me, and it started to rub me with a soft cloth. I couldn't see it, but I recognized its smell. This alien had pulled the covering from my nose when I first arrived.

Some of my fear concerning this invasion was lessening. This creature had helped me, and the vigorous rubbing felt wonderful. The smaller biped was busy drying my mom with a big soft rag, and it was talking to her, nonstop.

You are such a good mother, Sandy. I heard it say.

Big news flash, I thought. I might be new colt on the block, but I had already figured that out. I could feel its eyes, like twin laser beams, as it turned to look at me, and I had the feeling it knew what I was thinking.

Backyard Horse Tales 2

"Frosty and the Nightstalker

Excerpt from Chapter 2

The child was just six that spring, and he still believed in all the legends and ghost stories told by the people. That night was another dark one, making me hard to see, and my eyes caught the firelight. All that Little Wolf Saw were two glowing orbs moving toward him in the darkness, and he let out a howl that would have put a full-grown wolf to shame. He sure scared the poop out of me! I'd had more than enough of that game for the night.

Songbird must have squealed on her little brother. The next day, all the other children were teasing him relentlessly. Standing Bear took matters into his own hands and brought his little brother to see me in the daylight. Like I said before, I'm not spectacular by the light of day, nor at all frightening. I was just another young colt with a dark coat, a small star, a sock right ankle, snowflakes on my rump, and black spots there barely visible on my dark coat. In the winter I was almost black and my dark spots were invisible.

Standing Bear inched his sibling closer, and Little Wolf reached out his small hand. I lowered my head to get a better look at this small human. My first whiff of him told me he was the howler from a few nights ago. He petted my nose, with his small pudgy hand, then declared, "Mine!"

He came to see me every day, after that. An older family member accompanied Little Wolf on most of his visits, but sometimes he'd steal away and visit me by himself.

Several days of heavy rain kept him confined The rain was not very cold, but it melted much of the snow that was still high in the mountains. Melting snow increased the current of the river until it overflowed the banks. Mares wisely moved their foals farther from the rising water.

On the first sunny day, Little Wolf had escaped the watchful eyes of his mother and grandmother to come for an overdue visit. I heard cries of panic from the village, and turned to investigate the ruckus. The two women suddenly noticed that their charge was on the run toward the river. On most visits he came along a path that ran parallel to the river, but on that day the path was under water.

I watched the human drama as his mother ran to save her child form certain doom. The rascal took one look at his mother chasing after him, giggled, and picked up speed. I heard his mother let out a terrified screech when her son slipped and fell into the raging water.

At that point, I galloped as fast as I could to intercept the rambunctious little boy. He was able to grab hold of a partially submerged tree limb. His presence of mind allowed me the time I required. I plunged into the icy river and battled the current to reach him. I was becoming winded and my heart was pounding against my ribs as I swam upstream.

"Almost there, just a few more feet," I told myself as my strength threatened to fail me. I was so close. Then the child lost his grip! He began tumbling in the water and was headed in my direction. His little hand found purchase in my mane when he collided with me. The little imp scrambled onto my back and held to my mane for dear life.

River rescue illustration by Sandy Shipley
from
Frosty and the Nightstalker